Gypsy Spirit

By

Ellen Dugan

ACKNOWLEDGMENTS

As always, thanks to my family, friends, editors, and of course my beta readers:

Shawna, Becca, Katie, Erin and Terry.

Thank you to Kerr Cuhulain, for patiently and cheerfully answering my questions about police work and general procedure.

For the fans who fell in love with Nilah, Joseph, and Grandma Sabina. This one's for you!

"Ghosts seem harder to please than we are: it is as though they haunted for haunting's sake — much as we relive, brood, and smolder over our pasts."

-Elizabeth Bowen

PROLOGUE

Most women wouldn't have been able to run in stilettos, but Alicia James-Fogg wasn't merely any woman. She worked out twice a week with a personal trainer, played a mean game of tennis, and prided herself on her ability to put in an eight hour day in killer heels, all without chipping a nail. Alicia had worked hard to achieve the sort of lavish comforts and luxurious lifestyle most people could only dream of...

However at the moment, Alicia ran, and she ran for her life. As she sprinted through the November woods a litany of reasons why this couldn't be happening rushed through her mind. *She was beautiful, wealthy, and connected. These sorts of things simply didn't happen to people like her!*

She knew she'd never make it back into her car—so she leapt into the twilight cover of the trees and ran, as fast as her designer shoes would carry her.

Alicia nimbly dodged a low hanging branch, skid on the thick layer of fallen leaves, yet continued to tear down the darkened path. She wished desperately for her cell phone. But she'd dropped it behind her somewhere, along with her Coach bag.

The farther away she ran, the less she could see in the misty darkness. Alicia took a chance, ducked behind a large oak tree, and used the trunk for cover. Then she listened.

"Don't run from me, you bitch!" The furious voice sounded clearly through the woods.

She pressed her hands over her mouth to try and muffle the sounds of her own breathing.

He was coming closer, she realized, and now Alicia stopped breathing altogether.

A twig cracked on the other side of the tree and she bolted, pushing away from the shelter of the trunk. She managed about three steps before one of her designer high heels snapped.

She stumbled and was brought down.

Alicia James-Fogg screamed even as she was flipped over onto her back. She tried to fight off her attacker, but suddenly there was a terrible pressure around her throat. She clawed at the hands that were cutting off her air. Alicia twisted and thrashed, all to no avail. Her head was bounced brutally off the hard ground, once, then twice, and light seemed to explode in front of her eyes.

***

Alicia was wandering. First through the misty, late autumn woods...and eventually out and into the town proper. She walked around forever it seemed, yet no one noticed her, or would acknowledge her.

It was as if she were invisible.

She knew something was very wrong, but little else. Confused and alone she trudged along, until slowly she became more aware of herself. With that awareness came impatience.

Her clothes were a wreck and her Milano Blanc shoes were destroyed. She limped along, as one of her heels had broken off, and cursed the fact that she'd chipped several nails. *What would Maurice say when he saw her? What would Franklin think, when she didn't show up at home?*

*Franklin...*the name brought a sense of irritation when she considered it. While the name Maurice made her feel sad. However, the more Alicia James-Fogg tried to push for details, the less she could actually remember.

She felt a tug. An uncomfortable tightening at her midsection that seemed to pull her along. Intrigued, she followed the sensation, and slowly made her way up the back stairs of an old brick building off the town square...

CHAPTER ONE

I leaned against the doorframe dressed only in a black satin nightie and smiled as my lover grabbed a last cup of coffee before heading out for his day. *You have to admit,* I thought as I watched, *it was a hell of a view.*

Joseph Serafin, all buff and brawny six foot four inches of him, rested a hip against my kitchen counter, sampled his coffee and grinned back at me as I yawned. His denim blue shirt was still unbuttoned, allowing glimpses of a splendidly broad chest. His brown hair fell casually to the tops of his shoulders, while his beard was neatly trimmed. He looked exactly like what he was, a sexy man-beast...and he was all mine.

"Tired?" he asked, raising one eyebrow.

"You didn't let me get much sleep last night," I told him, and ran a hand through my long brown hair. It was probably sticking straight up in the air after having his hands in it most of the night…either from him smoothing it back from my face as he lavished kisses on me, or from yanking my head back by my hair as he held me firmly in place while he plundered.

God the man was good at plundering. I shuddered.

I saw movement out of the corner of my eye. Squash, my orange tabby cat, sat on the back of the couch, staring out the window through the break in the curtains. I felt a little tingle of sensation and checked again. *Was that a shimmer of light in the corner of the living room? What was causing that?*

My thoughts were distracted as Joseph turned to me, and I got a frontal view of him standing there in his jeans and unbuttoned shirt. My mouth watered. Even after a year together the man made my hormones go crazy. I calculated how much time he had before his first appointment of the day.

I stood up a little straighter, and one strap slid off my shoulder. "Oops," I said, as if I was surprised.

Joseph's gaze zeroed in. "Don't distract me, woman."

"Sorry." I shrugged and glanced down.

The nightie was starting to slither off the slope of my breast. The fabric clung, defying gravity, and the fact that I had big boobs to begin with only made the inevitable fall a little slower. I leaned back against the doorframe, stretched, and wondered what he would do.

He sent me a slow burning look out of those fabulous brown eyes. My belly clenched. *I knew that look.*

"Nilah." His voice was husky and low.

"Yes?" The nightie slid further down. I smiled, slowly.

The coffee cup hit the counter with a snap. In two steps he was in front of me. His mouth landed on mine, and I reached up and grabbed a handful of his long hair. He snagged me around the hips and lifted me. I wrapped my legs around his waist as he slung me to the old sturdy kitchen counter.

My shoulders hit the painted cabinets, and I groaned my delight into his mouth. While I tried to shove his shirt off his shoulders, I heard him unbuckling and unzipping. His mouth went from my mouth, to my throat, then he latched on to my breast.

"Joseph!" I reached back and wrapped my hands around his amazing ass, tugging him closer to me.

Standing between my thighs, he angled his hips and slammed into me. Exactly the way I liked it. He leaned in, holding still for a moment. Eye to eye, our hearts beat in unison, and I felt him stretch me tight as he pressed even deeper inside.

I let out a little gasp and that spurred him on. With a deep growl, he bent my knees further apart and began to thrust. I heard a crash as a few dishes were knocked from the counter to the floor, and the thump of my back hitting the cabinets as we took each other.

It wasn't long before I was shouting from my orgasm, and his release soon followed. We sprawled there and fought to catch our breath. Our eyes met, we grinned at each other, and began to laugh.

"Damn it Nilah, I'm going to be late," he grumbled.

"I didn't do anything," I said. "I was only standing there."

"Ha!" he laughed, and rubbed his beard across the sensitive skin of my breasts.

I shrieked and yanked his ear in retaliation. In revenge, he bit down on the upper slope of my breast and began to suck.

"Don't you dare give me a hickey!" I said, trying not to laugh.

He lifted his head and I felt the slight sting. "Just marking my territory." He dropped a playful kiss on my mouth and released me.

"Barbarian," I teased him.

Joseph walked over to the bathroom to clean up. I stayed put on the counter with my legs dangling off the side and tried to talk myself into moving.

I eventually managed to sit up straight and tug my nightie back down over the tops of my thighs. Joseph strolled out of the bathroom, all buttoned up. He tugged his boots on, gathered up his things in record time, grabbed his jacket and stopped to give me a kiss. I wrapped my fingers in his hair and held on. He lingered over the kiss long enough that I thought maybe he might stay.

I made a sound of disappointment when he stepped away.

He headed for the door, stopped and glanced over his shoulder. "I want you waiting for me just like that, when I get home tonight."

I raised my eyebrows. "Really? Is that an order or a request?"

"Order." He grinned.

"And if I don't?" I asked tartly.

The smile he sent me was devastating. "There will be *consequences*." He drew the last word out.

My stomach quivered. "Oh yeah?" I tossed my head at the challenge. "Is that a threat or a promise?"

"Both." He winked at me, grabbed the mini cooler that held his lunch, and let himself out the door.

I swung my legs for a moment, eased down from the counter, and headed to the bathroom to shower and clean up. Afterwards, I wrapped myself in a plush robe and fished out the disinfectant wipes from under the kitchen sink to wipe down the counter top.

Humming to myself, I threw the wipes in the garbage and picked up the dishes that had been knocked over during our romp. I straightened and headed towards the living room. What I saw there had me screaming in horror.

Alicia James-Fogg, my former boss, and the richest, biggest bitch in town, stood scowling at me...and she didn't look good. Her silk blouse was rumpled and stained. Her hair was a mess, and she was deathly pale.

I pressed my hands to my galloping heart. "What in the holy hell are *you* doing here?"

"I need your help," Alicia said, her voice raspy.

"How did you get in?" I demanded.

"I'm not sure..."

"Get out of my house!" I snapped.

"I can't," Alicia whined. "I don't even know how I got here."

I marched over, intending to grab the woman by the arm and throw her bodily out the door—and my hand went right through her shoulder.

A chill ran down my back. "Oh shit," I said, recoiling from the spirit.

"What's going on?" she said, sounding more shocked than me. "I've been wandering around for days, trying to find someone to help me...and I found myself drawn here." Alicia's bottom lip trembled. "Am I a ghost?"

I tossed my hands in the air. "Bingo! She got it right on the first try, folks!"

"I'm dead, then." Alicia looked around forlornly.

"I thought I had the place warded against roaming spirits," I groused. "You shouldn't be able to get in."

"Why am I *here*?" she wanted to know. "I don't understand how I got here."

"Probably because I'm the *only* one who can communicate with you."

"That can't be right," Alicia argued. "I don't even like you."

"Back at ya, baby," I snapped. A ghastly thought suddenly occurred to me. "How long have you actually been here?"

"For a while..." she said, turning up her nose. "You were too busy with that disgusting display to notice."

Now I was truly horrified. "You *watched* us, you perv?"

"Not by choice." She crossed her arms over her chest. "The kitchen counter? Really Nilah. That is so low class."

"Get out!" I pointed towards the door.

"I tried!" Alicia's bottom lip appeared to tremble. "I'm afraid I might be stuck here."

"Not for long if I have anything to say about it."

My name is Nilah Stephanik. I come from a long line of *Polska Roma* fortune tellers, mystics, and psychics. I'd always thought I had no occult talents of any kind...that is until about a year ago.

That was when I learned the hard way to be very careful what you wish for. Because it turns out that I'm a medium, and unfortunately, I can communicate with the dead.

Whether I want to or not.

***

For a hideously long few minutes, my former

boss and I stood staring at each other. "Okay, then," I said, and marched over to the large hutch in my living room. I pulled down a glass jar full of bay leaves and dropped three dried leaves in a ceramic bowl. I grabbed a lighter, intending to light them.

The flame that shot out of the end of the lighter was a bright blue. I gasped at seeing the color, but held the flame to the dried leaves anyway. The bay leaves caught immediately, releasing their fragrant smoke. "Spirit be gone, you are not welcome here," I chanted. "By the power of three, my home will be clear." For good measure, I held out the smoking bowl in Alicia's general direction.

According to my Witch-friend Christy, doing this would drive any roaming spirits out of the home. I repeated the charm a second time, waving the smoke around my apartment as Christy had taught me. The smoke made Alicia flinch, but she didn't disappear. In fact, she began to wail and cry. Loudly.

The sound was like fingernails on a chalkboard. It was so terrible that I dropped the bowl, which broke in two as it hit the hardwood floor. "Stop!" I yelled, clamping my hands over my ears.

"Don't do that!" Alicia sobbed. "I can't stand the smell!"

"Then get out!" I said, scooping up the smoldering leaves with one half of the bowl.

"No, no, no, no!" she cried, and the sound of it made me feel like something was tearing at my heart.

Clutching my chest with one hand, I dumped the mess into the kitchen sink. "Fuck this," I decided. If there was one person who would know how to get rid of my unwanted house-guest it would be my grandmother, the incomparable Madame Sabina.

Alicia continued to wail, and I ran for help. With my robe flying, I rushed down the steps to my grandmother's apartment. I glanced over my shoulder once, discovered that the spirit was right behind me, and increased my pace.

"*Babcia*!" I burst through her door and spotted her drying dishes in the kitchen. "I need your help!"

"Nilah!" My grandmother spun around in alarm. "What has happened? Are you hurt?"

"Look!" I pointed to where Alicia James-Fogg stood, crying right inside the door.

"What are you pointing at?" She stepped closer and the jar candle that was burning on her kitchen table flared, its flame turning a bright blue. My *babcia* froze in her tracks.

"Do you see her too?" I asked.

"No, but a blue candle flame warns of an unwanted spirit, and I *can* feel the cold spot." My grandmother tossed a dishtowel aside and made a gesture with both hands. "*Duch*, you are not welcome here!"

"Please!" Alicia begged, but she was blown right out the apartment door.

Muttering Polish under her breath, my grandmother stomped forward and slammed the door smartly. "To banish something, you have to mean it," she said, raising an eyebrow at me. "*Wnucka*, you must stand firm. Show no uncertainty to the *upiór*."

"Ooh-peeorra?" I tried to sound it out. "Please tell me that does *not* mean vampire!"

Babcia glared at me. "No in English it means, specter...or ghoul."

"Well I tried to banish her, like Christy

taught me."

"Ah, the *dobra czarownica,* your friend from the *magia* shop." Babcia nodded. "Yes, I remember."

"But the spirit started crying, and the sound was horrible!" I folded my arms over my chest. "It actually hurt to hear it."

"For you, yes, I suppose it would." My grandmother tugged me along and pushed me into a chair in her living room. "Did you know the woman in life?"

"Unfortunately, I did," I said. "It's Alicia James-Fogg my former boss and co-owner of Fogg Funeral Home."

My grandmother clamped a hand over mine. "The news. This morning. She is missing, they said."

"Well lucky me," I said sourly. "I've found her."

"Nilah, her *body* is not found."

"Oh," I said. "Ick." My grandmother and I exchanged a long glance. "Do you think she had an accident?" I asked quietly.

My grandmother pursed her lips. "I wouldn't think so..."

"Ghosts are often the victims of a violent crime," I muttered to myself. Even through the closed door, I could hear Alicia making a racket outside on the porch. I couldn't bear it, and I covered my ears.

My grandmother gently tugged my hands away. "You can still hear her?"

"Yeah, I feel this..." I searched for the correct words. "It's like a tearing at my heart, sort of sensation." I cringed. "Like if I don't go and answer her, it's only going to get worse."

My grandmother raised her brows. "You should go. Answer."

I nodded in agreement and rose to my feet. I stomped over to the door and whipped it open. "What?" I asked rudely.

"I think someone killed me!" Alicia announced.

"What, a *nice* lady like you?" I asked acidly. "Who'da thunk it?"

"I—" Alicia paused. "I can't remember much...I don't think I had an accident, though. It's all very confusing."

"What does she say?" *Babcia* wanted to know.

"That she thinks someone killed her, but her memories are confused," I relayed to my grandmother.

"What are you going to do about this?" Alicia demanded.

"What am *I* going to do?" I repeated.

"Yes, you!" She actually stomped her foot.

I eyeballed the ghost of the woman I thoroughly despised. "Don't know. I'll get back to you," I said, and shut the door in Alicia's face.

"Nilah," my grandmother struggled against a laugh. "That was unkind."

"Well, that may have been rude," I said, going back to the couch. "But I have to say it was one of the most satisfying moments of my adult life."

"You must tell someone that she has passed over."

"Who would believe me?" I asked.

"Beth would." My grandmother nodded at her own suggestion.

Beth Dustin, my boss and friend, was the owner of Danvers Paranormal Investigations. I'd been managing her office for a year and consulting with her on cases for the past six months—whenever they needed a medium. "Maybe Beth *would* know what to do," I murmured, thinking it over.

"Start with Beth," my grandmother recommended.

"Well I'm sure as hell not calling the police and telling them Alicia James-Fogg is suddenly floating around my apartment spying on Joseph and me having sex!" I heard my own words and bit my tongue. "Sorry, *Babcia*."

"The *duch,* was there this morning, then?"

"*Duch*?"

"Ghost," my grandmother translated.

"I suppose...Wait," I said. "How did you know about this morning?"

She pointed up to the ceiling. "I heard you two go after each other in the kitchen earlier."

"Oh my god!" I pressed my hands to my cheeks, mortified.

My grandmother laughed at my reaction. "*Kochaine*, I am aware that you have a healthy sex life. Hearing you two brought back memories of the days when your grandfather and I would—"

"Stop!" I cut her off.

"Young people," she said, roaring with laughter. "You always think you invented the sex."

I shook my head. "I am not swapping 'the sex' stories with my grandmother. No way!"

"No?" She grinned and reached for my hand. "Then settle down, and I will tell you what else you can do to keep the spirit out of your apartment."

I gave her fingers a squeeze. "Thanks, *Babcia*."

CHAPTER TWO

The ritual worked—sort of. Alicia Fogg-James' spirit could no longer get inside my apartment, but that didn't mean that I'd managed to banish her from my life. I came to this unfortunate discovery as I opened my door, preparing to leave for work later that morning.

Alicia was lurking on the landing, waiting to pounce, and she was furious. "Nilah Stefanik," she began, "how dare you!"

"It's pronounced Nile-ah. Not *nilla* like the cookie," I corrected the mistake, automatically. "And damn it, I banished you! You shouldn't still be here!"

She folded her arms and glared. "You and that old Gypsy woman can keep me out of your homes, but I'm not going anywhere until you help me."

"That 'old Gypsy woman' is my grandmother, and you will speak respectfully of her, or I will kick your ass." I pointed as I spoke, but got too close. My finger met with a cobwebby, cold sensation. "Ack!" I yanked my hand back.

Alicia seemed as surprised as I was by the discovery. "Well, that's interesting," she said softly in a considering tone.

"That felt *nasty*." I shook my hand off.

"So, you can't touch me, physically."

"Who would want to?" I shot back.

Alicia pressed a dramatic hand to her chest. "I'm simply grateful for whatever small mercies god has given me at this trying time."

I stood in my doorway, amazed at the arrogance of the woman. "May I remind you that you're basically, cursed?"

Alicia shrank back. "That's a horrible thing to say."

"You're the one roaming the earthly plane—instead of going on to the afterlife," I pointed out. "I think that speaks volumes of what god thinks of you."

"I never liked you," Alicia hissed.

"And you are a bigoted, rich snob," I said, careful to keep my voice down. The last thing I needed was someone to stroll down the back alley and see me talking to thin air. Deliberately, I locked the door and walked past the sulking spirit. I almost tripped when she materialized right in front of me at the bottom of the outdoor steps.

"You have to help! This can't happen to me, I'm an important woman in town. I simply refuse to accept this as my fate!"

Which is probably why she was still here, I realized. *She had refused to accept her fate.* "I'm sorry that you died." I tried for a neutral tone of voice. "But I don't know what you expect *me* to do about it."

"Maybe I was murdered. Perhaps, you're the only one who can find my killer and bring them to justice!"

I rolled my eyes. "Oh my god. This is not an episode of *Murder She Wrote.*"

"But it's not fair!" she wailed, and the sound made me grimace.

"Karma's a bitch," I pointed out. "Maybe

you should have kept that in mind while you were alive."

"Well, I..." Alicia trailed off and looked pathetic.

I sighed. "Alicia, I'm not sure what I *can* actually do to help you."

Alicia tilted her head to the side. "Do you need me to apologize first?"

"It wouldn't hurt." I pulled my long burgundy sweater closed against the chilly breeze. "Probably be good for you."

"I'm sorry!" Alicia cried. "I'm sorry for every mean thing I ever said about you."

"Go on." I tapped my foot and waited expectantly.

"I'm very sorry I had Franklin fire you. I'm sorry I called your family trashy. *Babcia,* is that your grandmother's name?"

"*Babcia* is Polish for grandmother," I explained. "Her *name* is Sabina."

"Oh, the old fortune teller in town. I didn't know you two were actual blood family." Alicia put a hand to her hair and tried to straighten her coiffure. "Well, I mean, one assumes that you're all related somehow, anyway..."

I sucked in a breath at the insult, but she barreled along.

"Sabina has a much nicer place than I expected for a Gypsy. Of what I could see for the second I was inside her home." She nodded, pleased with her own observations. "I wouldn't have thought your kind capable of such good taste."

"Wow," was about all I could manage.

Alicia seemed to clue in. "Oh, I'm sorry. I didn't mean to offend." She dipped her head, as if repentant. A second later her head snapped back up. "There, I apologized. *Now* will you help me?"

"Unbelievable." *Just when I was starting to feel a little sorry for her...*I shook my head and turned away.

"You can't abandon me. I'm a soul in need!"

"There's not a single person in town who would believe that you have—had a soul." I said, stepping around her. "Bye Felicia!" I snapped my fingers in the 'bitch please' style and walked right to my car.

I started the engine and managed to keep from flinching when she materialized in the passenger seat.

"My name is *Alicia*," she said through her teeth. "Not. Felicia."

"Fuck my life." I dropped my head to the steering wheel in defeat.

"Language." Alicia sniffed, as if offended.

I hadn't truly expected it to be that easy to get rid of her...but I'd hoped. Resigned, I backed up my car and decided to take my 'problem' to my boss.

"Where are we going?" Alicia made a motion as if reaching for her seatbelt.

"I wouldn't worry about a seatbelt," I said, belatedly snapping my own in place.

"Why not?" Alicia wanted to know.

Somehow I managed to hold back an inappropriate giggle. *No laughing at the dead woman who didn't seem to understand that she didn't need to buckle herself in.* I cleared my throat instead. "It's not like you really need it now."

"Oh." Alicia folded her hands in her lap. "You may proceed, Nilah" she said grandly.

"I'm *not* your damned chauffer," I reminded her.

Alicia inclined her ghostly head. "Yet, you are driving me."

Silently, I clenched my teeth. If anyone would know how to proceed with my 'I-have-an-obnoxious-ghost-following-me-around situation', it would be Beth. All I had to do was get to the office.

The office was on the bottom floor of a large three story home. It sat back from the street in a pretty residential area and was painted deep gray with bright white trim. Only a small and discreet sign announced it to be the headquarters for DPI: Danvers Paranormal Investigations.

As I pulled around back, I heaved a sigh and glared at my unwanted passenger. She'd badgered me during the entire drive. Non-stop.

"And what about my dog? Who will take care of him?" Alicia wondered.

"You have a dog?" I managed to get a few words in edgewise.

"Royal is a champion," she said. "Best in show, as one would expect. He's very delicate and requires only the finest of care."

He was probably a yappy little purse dog, I

figured, and gripped the steering wheel tighter as her monologue continued.

"I was supposed to host the tennis club at our house this weekend—I'm president of that, obviously. What will they do without me? No one else is capable of the sort of organization required..."

And on and on she went. Never once mentioning her husband. Only whining about the ladies at the club, her various committees, and of course—her champion dog.

Torn between nausea and a headache, I gathered up my things, nodded as she continued her litany of complaints, and headed for the back entrance of the house. I was pretty sure Beth had her home warded against spirits, ghouls, and the shambling dead. Not that I'd ever seen any zombies personally...but she *was* friends with Christy too, and a few more of the local Witches. Besides, Beth had insisted that the place was impenetrable, otherwise I would never have been able to comfortably work there.

I probably should have mentioned the whole impenetrable thing to my ghostly tag-a-long but

I really wanted to see what would happen. I opened the door and began to cross the threshold, and when Alicia tried to follow me in, she actually ricocheted off the house. Hard enough that her words were forcibly cut off on impact. She ended up in the middle of the backyard under a huge old oak tree. And she was livid.

"Sweet," I said, absolutely delighted by the results of the wards. "Stay put Alicia," I called over to her. "And let me see what I can find out."

"Don't you dare—" she began.

Once I crossed the threshold completely, I couldn't even hear her anymore. My shoulders dropped in relief at the blessed silence, and I shut the door.

Note to self: Find out who did the mojo on Beth's place and have them do the same on mine.

"Good morning!" Beth called out.

I discovered my boss leaning against the far counter. Today the blonde wore jeans and a gray sweatshirt that read, *Ghost Hunters Do It In Haunted Houses*.

"Who were you talking to out there?" she asked, and took a sip out of her coffee mug.

I set my things down on my desk before answering. "Beth," I said. "I am about to impose on our friendship."

"That sounds ominous!" Her eyes danced above her cup. "Did you kill somebody? Let me go get a shovel and a tarp."

I winced. "Well actually... I don't know quite how to begin."

Beth set her mug down on the filing cabinet. "What's wrong?" she asked.

"You were one of the first people to ever see me use my medium abilities, and you became my friend anyway...but this is way beyond anything I've experienced so far."

"Tell me."

"Do you remember my former boss, Alicia James-Fogg?"

Beth's shoulders stiffened. "Yes, I do. Everyone's least favorite society snob has been missing for three days. The police are starting to think foul play. This morning, they found her car. It was abandoned a few counties over."

"Did Rick tell you that?"

"No. He doesn't tell me the details of his cases," she said of her cop boyfriend. "Actually, I heard it on the morning news."

"Alicia James-Fogg *has* died," I said quietly.

Beth tilted her head considering my words. "Is that your professional opinion as a medium, or a simply a hunch?"

I crossed my arms over my chest. "Beth, her spirit showed up at my apartment this morning. *Babcia* showed me how to banish her, so she can't get back inside...but she's been following me around everywhere, since I stepped out my front door."

Beth's smile slid away. "Oh my god."

"She's out in the yard." I hooked a thumb towards the window. "Whatever mo-jo your Witch friends did on this place had her bouncing off the house like a rubber ball. And for that—I'm grateful. The woman hasn't shut up since I left my apartment."

Beth went to the window. "She's out there now?"

I double checked. "Yes. She's under that big tree and pacing back and forth. But seriously, she's like a dog on a leash that I can't drop.

What should I do?"

Beth bolted for her office and ran back in a moment later with an EMF meter and a mini EVP recorder. She grabbed my arm. "Show me where she is, exactly!"

I was dragged along, and as soon as Beth opened the back door Alicia's voice was audible to me once again. "She's still bitching," I muttered.

Beth pulled me across the back porch. "You couldn't hear her while you were inside the office?" She switched on her recorder.

"No. Like I said, I want your Witch friends to come over to my place and fix me up. Because banishing her skinny ass only went so far… Now I'm thinking an exorcism. The whole bell, book, and candle, whatever it takes."

"Sure, sure." Beth towed me down the steps and across the leaf strewn grass. "Take me right to her."

"Alicia," I called over. "This is Beth, she wants to help. If you can, try and talk to her."

"Well, finally," Alicia flipped her tangled hair. "I assume she is competent? Because her fashion sense is deplorable."

"Don't be a bitch, Alicia," I said.

Beth made wide sweeps with her monitor, and it started to beep with a louder and faster pitch when she aimed it in Alicia's direction. "Check out that energetic spike!" Beth sounded thrilled.

"There." I positioned Beth, adjusting her slightly. "She's right in front of you now."

Alicia puckered up. "Tell your friend, that if she doesn't stop waving that light thing around in my face, I'm going to leave."

"Do you promise?" I snarked back.

"What?" Beth looked at me, confused.

"Alicia doesn't like the EMF meter." I relayed the information.

The lights on the meter went from green to bright red. "Awesome," Beth blew an appreciative whistle, but lowered the meter and began asking questions in a sort of one sided interview.

After a few moments, Alicia scowled at me. "At least you had the courtesy to bring me to a professional."

"Beth can help you, Alicia." *I was pretty sure of that.* "If you'll let her."

Alicia let out an aggrieved sigh. "I suppose I should let her try."

I had no polite response, so I stepped back, hoping that any responses from Alicia would be recorded.

CHAPTER THREE

After Beth finished up her session, Alicia's image slowly disappeared, becoming more and more transparent until I could no longer see, or even hear her.

"She's faded—I mean her *image* faded away," I said to Beth.

"She probably burned through a lot of energy trying to communicate," was Beth's answer as we headed back inside. "But she's determined." Beth nodded. "I bet she comes back."

"Well at least I can't hear her blather on anymore." I shrugged when I said it, but in the back of my mind, I was uneasy.

I began to understand why, when Beth played back the EVP session for me a few hours later. She'd actually caught a few of Alicia's words on the tape.

Deplorable, was the first one. I explained to my friend that Alicia's comment had been about Beth's outfit, and she nodded and wrote it down. The word *try*, was the only part picked up from: *I suppose I should let her try*. And the last words were a direct response to, where are you? Answer: *lost*.

And finally: *help me*.

Those last two words caught on the EVP session made my skin crawl.

"This is incredible." Beth blew out a long breath that had her bangs fluttering back.

"So what's our next step?"

"I think I'm going to call Rick and let him know what's in the wind," Beth decided.

"What should I do?" I looked out the window. "I don't see her out there."

Beth rested her hand on my shoulder. "For now, stay inside. Like I said, there's a good chance she'll reappear."

"You are such a comfort to me," I said dryly.

"One does what they can." Beth chuckled. "At least in here she won't be able to hound you."

"Good point," I agreed. "I suppose I could go ahead and update the website and put the new ads in place." A thought occurred to me. "Would you mind if I called Christy? I'd like to get her opinion too."

"Sounds like a plan." Beth nodded. "Let me know if you need anything else. Or if there's a change."

"Okay boss." I flashed a smile as she left, honestly admiring her matter-of-fact handling of the situation.

I managed to put in a solid days work; answering the phones, working on the website, and setting up an investigation for the following week. I called Christy on my lunch break, and she agreed to come over and help me reinforce the wards on my home. I felt silly, but I did check out the window a few more times during the day, and Alicia was still nowhere to be seen. Finally at five o'clock, I printed the files from the Danvers county online records on a property up for paranormal investigation and tucked it into a folder.

I went to take it to Beth and walked in on my friend who was currently trapped against her office wall by a very attractive police officer. Officer Casper had Beth's hands pinned above her head and was kissing the daylights out of her.

"Ooops," I laughed, and they jolted apart.

"Hi, Nilah." Rick turned, and a faint blush rode across his cheeks.

"Sorry to interrupt." I grinned at them.

Beth smiled and waved me in. "Are those the files on the Lockwood property?"

I handed them over. "Yeah, I've got copies of the records from the previous owners all the way back to the 1800's, when it was first built."

"I filled Rick in on today's events," Beth said as she scanned the papers.

Rick tugged at his collar. "We were just listening to the EVP session."

"Listening to an EVP session?" I said, straight faced. "Is *that* what you're calling it these days?" I crossed my arms and leaned against the doorframe. "Seemed more like I'd interrupted a strip search."

"Nah, it was more like a thorough frisking," Beth joked.

"Come to think of it..." I pressed my hand

dramatically to my forehead. "I am detecting a little *friskiness* in the atmosphere."

Keeping up the puns, Beth wiggled her eyebrows at Rick. "I wasn't even resisting."

Rick's lips twitched. "Well, Beth is a person of interest. To me."

I smiled at his comeback. I genuinely liked Rick Casper. He was kind, caring, had a quiet sense of humor, and was generally enthusiastic about paranormal investigations. Plus he made my friend very happy.

It was Rick who had been the officer on duty that fateful day Beth and I had met. The afternoon when her grandmother's ghost, Lizzie Samuels, had turned the Fogg Funeral home's meeting office into shambles, while trying to get everyone's attention.

"Nilah." Rick met my eyes. "If you get any more information, of *any* kind about Alicia James-Fogg, please contact me right away."

"I will," I promised. I said my goodbyes to the couple and gathered up my things. I let myself out and stayed on the back steps for a moment, checking for Alicia. But she was gone.

I drove home silently, but didn't feel

relieved. Instead I felt anxious, like I was waiting for the other shoe to drop. My apartment seemed very quiet, so I flipped on the radio, started some water for pasta, tossed a bag salad, and thought about the day's events. Joseph let himself in the front door, and Squash made a beeline for him, pouncing on his boots.

Joseph scooped up the tabby and draped him over his shoulders as he typically did in the evenings. The cat settled in with a purr, and I mentally prepared myself for the talk I knew we had to have.

"Hi handsome." I smiled at him.

"Hi." He leaned over and planted a firm kiss on my lips. "You're not waiting for me on the counter, as ordered."

I snorted out a helpless laugh. "I forgot about that. I've been a little distracted today."

"Well, at least you're cooking dinner." Joseph teased, knowing full well I'd retaliate for the comment.

I waited until he moved past, and I picked up a towel from the counter. I flipped the towel, took aim, and fired. The terrycloth made a satisfactory snap against his butt.

"Hey!" He laughed, and playfully snatched the towel from me.

"We need to talk," I said as he went to put his things away. "Something happened today that you should know about."

He straightened from where he'd stowed his cooler and studied my face carefully. "Medium stuff?"

I sighed. "Yes."

"Is it serious?"

"It has the potential to be," I admitted, and slid the pasta into the boiling water.

Joseph rested a large hand on my shoulder. "Let me clean up and then we can talk."

"Okay," I said.

As my lover went to hit the showers, I set the table. Eyeballing the wine rack above my fridge, I selected a bottle of red and poured us each a glass. I had a feeling we would need it.

***

That evening, my dreams were haunted by misty woods that felt foreboding and creepy. The restless night had me staggering out of bed the following morning and irritated that I wasn't able to sleep in on my day off. I leaned against the kitchen counter, waiting for my tea to brew, while Joseph packed his lunch for the day. Squash sat beside me on the counter and batted my arm. I yawned and gave the cat a good chin scratching.

When the cat suddenly whipped his head around and let out a low yowl, I flinched back. "What's wrong, Squash?"

The cat leapt off the counter and went to the back door. He began pacing in front of it. Curious, I followed the tabby. As I drew nearer I heard a distinct scratching noise coming from outside. "Friend or foe?" I whispered to myself, attempting to get a psychic impression or *sense* for whatever was on the other side of the door. I sucked in a deep breath and held my hands out to test for any possible negative vibrations.

"Nilah?" Joseph called to me. "What are you doing?"

Caught, I flushed a bit from embarrassment. "Nothing, apparently." I shrugged away my disappointment. *Once again my magickal talents were a bust. Either that or there was nothing paranormal out there on my back landing.* Irritated, I yanked the door open and saw...nothing. Only the pair of colorful glass lanterns that swung gently in the breeze. I rolled my eyes at myself for even trying anything remotely metaphysical, and then something brushed against my bare toes.

I glanced down, saw a pair of bulging black eyes, and screamed.

Joseph was at my side an instant later, pushing me back from whatever threat might be on the landing. "For god's sakes woman!" Joseph started to laugh. "It's only a dog!" He bent over, scooped up the dog and brought him inside, shutting the door behind him.

"That's not a dog!" I insisted. "It's a bug-eyed, hideous creature!"

The dog wriggled, licked Joseph's chin, and let out a happy, sharp bark. "It's a pug," Joseph explained, while Squash circled around with a low hiss, trying to assess the invader to his territory.

"Squash doesn't like him," I said. "He shouldn't be in the house."

"He's got a collar." Joseph reached for the

tags that dangled, while the dog did his best to win over my man. "Where did you come from, boy?" Joseph addressed the pug, who clearly sensed an ally and did his best to pull out all his cute doggy moves.

"We're not keeping it," I warned Joseph, not liking the goofy grin on his face.

"Of course not," Joseph agreed. "But the least we can do is try and contact his owners."

Resigned, I sat on the couch next to Joseph while he checked the ID tags on the affectionate pug's collar.

"There's a vaccination tag from a vet, with a number to the office." Joseph said. "We can call that later and find out who his owners are. Wait, he has a name tag too." Joseph accepted more dog kisses to his face while he read the tags. "Royal," he announced. "Silly name for a dog, if you ask me."

"What did you say?" I asked, feeling the blood drain from my face.

"His name is Royal." Joseph gave the creature who now sat contentedly in his lap a pat on the head.

"Joseph." I put my hand on his arm. "Alicia's

ghost told me she had a dog named Royal."

The dog whined and dropped his head on his paws and seemed forlorn.

"Do you belong to Alicia?" I asked it, and in answer, the dog lifted its head and stared at me. Those massive eyes would have melted an iceberg. "Did she send you to me?" I asked, and the dog gave another little whine.

"What are you thinking?" Joseph asked quietly.

"That somehow she sent the dog here." I ran my hand over the sad dog's little button ears. "She kept talking about him yesterday."

"The Fogg's live clear across town," Joseph pointed out. "How in the hell did the little guy get all the way over here?"

"Maybe he sensed that she'd been here..."

"Is that possible?" Joseph wanted to know.

"Maybe. I mean it's not any weirder than me talking to spirits."

Squash popped back up. He rested his front paws on the couch and began to sniff the pug that sat happily in Joseph's lap. I expected a free for all, but to my surprise the tabby hopped in my lap as if to stake his claim. Royal lifted his head, began to wag his tail and leaned forward to sniff Squash.

Squash put out his paw immediately against the pug's face, stopping Royal in mid lean. They stayed like that for a few seconds, Squash holding the dog off, and when Royal licked Squash's paw, the cat relented.

The dog yawned and closed his eyes. He was asleep and snoring in seconds.

While I got dressed for the day I did my best to keep Squash and Royal in separate rooms, but to my surprise it wasn't necessary. Squash settled in on top of the fridge and kept an eye on our visitor, while the dog snored away on my couch.

After a stern warning not to do anything stupid in regards to my involvement with the ghost, Joseph fashioned me a leash out of the belt from my robe. It was slightly ridiculous, but at least I could get the little beastie downstairs without carrying him. Comfortable in my black shirt, jeans and tennis shoes, I pulled on a long duster length sweater in amethyst purple and took myself and the dog downstairs to the psychic parlor. I wanted my grandmother's opinions on the latest developments.

Royal followed politely on his makeshift leash, and when I let myself in the back door of the parlor he sat by my feet while I locked the door. As I started towards the sales floor, he stayed neatly at my side.

I looked down at him, impressed with his manners. "She said you were a champion."

Royal sat and flashed a doggy grin. He lifted a paw to shake.

"Cut that out." I grumbled, but took the offered paw anyway. "Stop trying to be cute."

He bounced backwards and gave a little bark. His whole backside was wagging.

"Okay, okay, you win." I smiled and patted his head. "Now let's go talk to *Babcia*."

Royal pranced beside me and out into the shop. I'd barely finished greeting my grandmother, before my sister Vanessa spotted the dog.

She promptly and completely lost her mind over him. "Oh aren't you adorable?" Vanessa dropped to her knees, uncaring of her expensive clothes, and cuddled the dog.

While I tried to explain how I'd found him, she made loud kissy noises over Royal. It sent him into a joyous wriggle. She scooped him up and took him to sit behind the front counter with her.

I don't think she's that affectionate with her own little girl," I said, wryly.

Babcia snorted out a laugh. "Nilah, you exaggerate." As my sister began to speak in high pitch baby talk to Royal, my grandmother winced. "Do you know who the dog belongs to?"

"I'm pretty sure he belonged to Alicia James-Fogg."

My grandmother's eyes went sharp. Now I was addressing the professional psychic, Madame Sabina. "Yes, I agree." She picked up on my thoughts. "I do believe her spirit sent the dog to you."

"Why me?" I sighed.

"Why do *you* think she did?" She raised her brows.

"Because she was worried about it?" I said, pretending an interest in the display of crystal balls on a nearby shelf.

"That feels right." My grandmother nodded.

I lowered my voice. "As far as I can tell it's the *only* thing she really cared about...other than herself."

"Love is a powerful motivator," my grandmother said. "I will throw some cards over the situation this afternoon, after my morning appointments, and let you know what I discover."

I glanced towards my sister as she cooed over the pug, and movement caught my eye through the shop's front window. There, standing right beneath the bright purple neon sign that advertised psychic readings, stood Alicia James-Fogg's spirit.

A few clients came in and unknowingly walked right past her. She motioned to me to come outside, and my heart sank.

Day off or not, I still had work to do.

CHAPTER FOUR

The clients opened the shop door, greeted my grandmother, and headed back to the parlor for their readings. I waved to them and went to my sister, making up some lame excuse about having to run errands. As I expected, she was more than happy to keep an eye on Royal. I'd barely made my way out the front door before the ghost appeared at my side.

"You've found him." Relief was plain in Alicia's voice.

I checked around, making sure no one was close enough to hear me speak. "Yeah, he's inside. My sister is spoiling him at the moment." I inclined my head and went around to the back of the building where we could speak without folks staring at what they would perceive as my one-sided conversation.

"He could see *and* hear me," Alicia said as she followed me to our little parking area. "Other than you, no one else can."

"Animals are often more in tune with the spirit world," I tried to explain.

"I wanted him to be safe." Alicia's eyes were huge and swam with tears. "Please, promise me, he can't go to a shelter!" Alicia insisted. "He's a champion."

Her raw emotions over that goofy dog had me struggling against tears. "I won't take him to a shelter. You have my word on that."

"You'll find him a good home?"

"I'll take care of it," I said, studying her. "Maybe now that you know your dog is safe, you can...you know...cross over?"

"No." she shook her head and her image was brighter, more defined. "I'm not ready yet. They're still a few things to take care of."

"Such as?" I asked, despite myself.

"You have to help them find me."

I sighed and leaned against the hood of my car. *Somehow, I knew this was coming.* "Alright," I said giving in to the inevitable. "Do you know where I should search?"

"I'm not in town," Alicia said, as if she was talking to herself.

"Then where are you?"

"The woods," Alicia frowned. "A park maybe. There's a lake and trees..."

I rolled my eyes. "Well that vagues it right up."

"I didn't drive far that day to meet Maurice..."

"Maurice?"

"My lover." Alicia attempted to fluff her hair.

"Shut the front door. Your lover's name was *Maurice*?"

"He's French and very sophisticated."

"And next to Franklin, he's probably a top suspect, if you were killed." I pointed out.

"No," she said. "Maurice loved me."

I noticed that she didn't say that her husband had loved her, and my stomach dropped. "Alicia." I cleared my throat. "If you can't recall the circumstances of your death, how can you be sure it wasn't Maurice?"

"I simply know."

I stood, studying her image. *Maybe she*

*wasn't really dead, maybe she was in a coma or something. But that would mean she'd sent her astral body to see me, and she wasn't a ghost at all...*My mind hurt just thinking about it.

"Get in your car," Alicia snapped.

"Aw, hell no. I'm not taking a road trip with a ghost."

"I think I can take you to my body."

That shut me up, and I chose my next words with care. "Are you sure you want to do this?"

"Yes." Alicia nodded.

I'd worked for the Fogg funeral home for a few months. Part of working for the funeral home had included a tour and an overview of the entire operation. I had seen a few bodies that weren't—I guess you'd say—*fresh*.

I nervously cleared my throat again. "You've been missing for *four* days Alicia."

"Exactly my point!" Alicia huffed impatiently. "If we don't find my body soon, I'll look horrible in my casket!"

I did a double take. "Huh?"

"One does want to present themselves well, even in death." Alicia brushed at her stained blouse. "I hope they pick out something nice to bury me in, hopefully my new cobalt blue suit from Paris."

And the bitch was back. "Every time I start to feel sympathy for you..." I trailed off.

"You don't understand. The suit was part of the fall collection. Everyone will be so envious when they see me in it!"

The woman was dead and all she thought about was her appearance, and people being jealous of her wardrobe? I shook my head at her vanity.

"What?" she asked.

"If I agree to do this, and we find you, will it help you cross over?"

"There's only one way to find out."

I shut my eyes and prayed for patience. "So where are we going?"

"Head to highway 114 and drive west."

Which is how I found myself driving west with a ghost riding shotgun. A short time later, I pulled into the little roadside park. It was quiet, secluded and empty of other vehicles. I'd never even known of its existence.

"What is this place?" I asked.

"It's where I usually met Maurice," Alicia

explained.

I turned off the engine, climbed out of the car, and scanned the parking lot. A small sign announced it as the Middleton Hiking Park. There were hiking trails posted on a big sign, and I was suddenly grateful I'd worn jeans and sneakers.

Alicia was no longer beside me. She was suddenly standing at the farthest edge of the parking lot. When she motioned for me to follow her, I hitched my purse over my shoulder, swallowed my unease, and silently padded across the asphalt.

"Hey Alicia," I said. "I'd like to point out that the hiking trails are on the *other* side of the parking lot."

"I didn't go on a hiking trail." Alicia rolled her eyes as if I were stupid for suggesting such a thing. "I jog on a treadmill like a normal person. I don't trek through the woods, like some heathen."

"Well why did you come all the way out here?" I asked, checking out the area. The leaves had mostly fallen and there was a nip in the air. There was a filtered light coming through the clouds, but there was no discernable hiking trail, or path.

"I ran here," Alicia said slowly as if she'd only now figured it out. "I think I ran away from someone."

"Who?" I asked. "Who did you run away from?"

"We have to hurry," she said, and zipped off further into the woods.

All at once, the reality of being out and alone in an unfamiliar location kicked in. I took a moment and pulled out my phone. "Better safe than sorry," I muttered. Selecting the compass app, I got my bearings and kicked a large patch of leaves clear, leaving a bare spot on the ground to mark my starting spot.

"Come on!" Alicia called impatiently and disappeared father into the woods.

"I probably should have told someone where I was going," I said to myself. "Not that I knew where *that* was, until after I'd arrived..."

I walked for about fifteen minutes, muttering to myself the entire way, and marked my trail however I could. Kicking large spots clear of leaves, I made directional arrows from fallen sticks that pointed the way out. It wasn't perfect, but at least I wouldn't get lost. I didn't think I would anyway.

My foot kicked against something, and it bounced forwards through the fallen leaves. I approached it slowly. "What the hell?" I muttered and bent down. It was a fancy purse, and finding it made my skin start to crawl.

I picked up a fallen stick. Using the heavy end of the branch, I looped it through the strap of the bag and lifted it clear of the leaves.

"Come on!" Alicia said, suddenly appearing beside me.

"Jesus!" I squealed and dropped the purse back to the ground. "You scared me half to death!" I glared at her.

"Leave it," Alicia insisted, "and follow me."

Reluctantly, I propped the branch up over the purse and hoped I'd be able to find it again. I checked to see where she'd gone and noticed that the trees were much thicker now. We were deep in the woods and alone. "No, this isn't creepy," I muttered under my breath. "Not at all."

I continued following my ghostly trail guide.

I'd estimated I'd been walking a good five more minutes when I ducked under a low branch and saw Alicia. She was standing about twenty feet away beside a large pine tree, and her shoulders were shaking. "Alicia?" I called over to her.

"Look at what he did!" she said.

I hurried closer and the smell was the first thing to hit me. Stopping in my tracks, I clamped a hand over my nose and mouth, and fought against the need to gag.

"How could someone do this?" Alicia sobbed, dropping to her knees in the leaves. "Just leave me here?"

The body was about five feet in front of me and partly concealed in leaves. Oddly the face wasn't covered at all. Its eyes were open. They were milky and staring up at the sky, forever frozen in time. "Oh, shit." I cringed and turned away, while Alicia began to wail in earnest.

I don't know what I'd expected. Traipsing through the woods following a pain-in-the-ass spirit was one thing. But I hadn't really thought about the reality of finding a body. *Her body,* I corrected myself silently. I psyched myself up, and forced myself to check again—to be sure.

It was horrible. The body was bloated, making the face appear distorted. There were dark patches and blisters on the skin, but it was definitely Alicia James-Fogg. I saw a few bright spots of color peeking out from the leaves...Alicia's coral nail polish. I squinted down at those little patches of color and realized her nails were trashed. They were ragged and broken.

Alicia's wails began to diminish and I glanced over in time to see that her image was fading. I lowered my hand from where I'd covered my nose and mouth. "I'll get help Alicia," I said, struggling against tears. "I'll have them take you home. I promise."

She looked up at me, nodded once, and was gone. Without warning, I was suddenly alone with the body. The only thing I could hear in the November woods was the occasional call of a bird and the rustle of falling leaves.

"Oh my god," I said to no one in particular. The breeze shifted and I got hit with the odor again. *God the smell!* I lurched back, managed about four steps, and threw up all over the trunk of a nearby oak tree.

***

Once I stopped heaving, I staggered farther away from the body. I pulled my cell phone out, considered dialing 911 and then wondered how in the hell I would explain myself. So I selected Beth's number from my contacts list instead.

"Hello?"

"Beth?" I said. "I'm going to need to borrow your boyfriend the cop."

"Huh?" Beth chuckled in confusion.

"I found Alicia James-Fogg's body."

"What?" Beth practically shouted. "You found the body? Where are you! Are you alright?"

"I threw up, but other than that, yeah."

"You threw up?"

"Yeah, I don't think I threw up on the body though." I said and half-gagged in reaction to my own words. I walked farther up wind and could hear Beth shouting for Rick Casper.

"Nilah?" Rick barked in the phone.

"I'm sorry to interrupt—" I began, lamely.

"Where are you?" Rick demanded. "Are you alone?"

"Yes. I am," I said.

"*Where* are you?" he asked again.

"Middleton Park," I said. "Rick, you need to send someone out to the Middleton Hiking Park."

Rick told me to stay on the line with Beth and he handed over the phone. "He's calling it in," Beth said. "Nilah stay calm. It's going to be alright."

I took a few shaky steps away from where I'd been sick and sat on the ground in a pile of leaves. "Tell Rick they can follow the trail. I marked my trail, I mean. Oh and I found a purse," I babbled into the phone.

"Sure, sweetie." Beth's voice was calm and soothing. "What color jacket do you have on Nilah?"

"It's a sweater," I said, confused by the question. "Dark purple. Why?"

I heard her relay the information, and spent the longest twenty minutes of my life sitting up wind of Alicia James-Fogg's body and waiting for the police to arrive.

I didn't turn my back on her remains. That seemed rude somehow. But I kept her in my peripheral vision and told myself to remain calm. Beth stayed on the phone with me the entire time, and when I finally heard the sirens, I made myself stand up and watch for the police officers.

I could hear them calling my name and I lifted my arm to wave. "I'm here!" I called back.

Officer Rick Casper was the first to arrive, and as soon as he reached me I found myself in a very firm bear hug.

"Hi Rick," I said in a shaky voice.

"Are you okay?" he asked, running his hands down my back.

Part of my mind wondered if he was patting me down. "I found her," I managed.

"You sure as hell did." He sounded resigned.

"I think I found her purse back a little ways," I said. "Well, I think it was her purse, I could be wrong..."

Rick handed me off to an EMT, and that man immediately tugged me farther away, while Rick barked out orders to the other officers.

"Hi, I'm Stan." A tall, muscular black man guided me over to sit on the ground. "How do you feel, Nilah?" He began to take my pulse.

"I'm fine," I protested. "Only a little embarrassed that I threw up."

"Don't be," Stan said, patting my wrist. "I've seen cops throw up at crime scenes lots of times."

Shit! His words had me reevaluating. *Crime scene. This was a crime scene. And I'd walked right through it.* I'd been so determined to get rid of Alicia's obnoxious ghost that I'd never even considered the true gravity of the situation.

My teeth began to chatter, and that annoyed the hell out of me. A while later Stan draped a blanket over my shoulders, made some comment about shock, and he led me out of the woods to the parking lot, where Beth was waiting.

"Nilah!" She gave me a firm hug and held on as I began to shake all over again. "What were you thinking coming out here by yourself?"

I tucked my head on her shoulder and hugged her back. "It just sort of happened."

Beth yanked back suddenly. "You did get sick, didn't you?"

"Yeah." I sniffled.

Beth began to dig in her purse. "Here, take this." She handed me a mint. "Your breath is terrible."

I popped it in my mouth. "Thanks."

"Was it really bad?" she asked me quietly. "The condition of the body?"

"I hope I never see anything like it again," I admitted.

In sympathy, Beth took my hand and held it.

They didn't let me leave, of course. I was interviewed by a police officer and then by another detective. At some point someone had called Joseph, and he wasn't too happy when he arrived at the park.

He grasped me by the shoulders, and picked me straight up off the hood of my car where I'd been sitting. "What were you thinking coming out here alone?" he demanded.

"That's exactly what I said!" Beth piped in.

"I'm sorry," I began, and my words were cut off by his firm kiss.

"Woman, you need a keeper." He blew out an

aggravated breath and pulled me in for a tight hug.

I hugged him back. "I thought if I found her," I whispered to him. "That maybe she'd finally leave me alone."

He pressed a gentle kiss to my forehead. "The cops are going to have a field day when you tell them how you found her body."

"I spoke to Rick yesterday," I reminded Joseph. "He knows Alicia's spirit has been following me around."

"You're damn lucky he's already seen you in action with the medium stuff before," Joseph pointed out.

"I know." I shuddered and then flinched when a couple of local news vans arrived at the park.

"Uh-oh," Beth said.

Before I could comment on that, the detective walked up. "Ms. Stefanik, I'm going to need you to come down to the station with me. We have a few more questions, and I'll need a formal statement."

"Of course." I nodded.

"Damn," Joseph sighed as the detective

gestured for me to follow him. "This is going to be a really *long* day."

CHAPTER FIVE

Joseph was right. I'd been interviewed, a third, and fourth time. And I'd given the same story to the new detectives as I had to the police officers on the scene. I told them the truth: That the spirit of Alicia James-Fogg had appeared to me, and I followed her directions.

I explained that her spirit had confided that she had been meeting her lover, Maurice, at the hiking park. And that she'd told me she had run away from someone. When her spirit had gone into the woods, I'd followed her, hoping that she would show me where to find her body.

Detective Tucker raised an incredulous eyebrow. "Why would you follow a ghost into the woods?" he scoffed.

"Because," I said as patiently as possible. "I

thought that if I did find her body and she was properly buried; maybe she would finally cross over and stop bothering me."

As you can imagine, my answer didn't go over especially well.

While I sat waiting, I saw Franklin Fogg being led down the hall by a different uniformed officer. It made my heart lurch to see him. He wasn't alone, a man in a suit followed him—probably his lawyer.

Then I had a nasty moment of panic wondering if *I* would end up needing a lawyer.

Eventually I was allowed to leave. I think the main reasons I hadn't ended up sitting in a cell was because they knew where I lived and worked, *and* they knew my family. Danvers is a small town, plus I had Rick to vouch for my mediumship abilities. So I'd been allowed to go home. With the caveat that I should *not* leave town.

When I stepped outside I almost wished they made me stay. There were reporters hanging around the station, and they'd bombarded me with all sorts of horrible questions on the way to Joseph's car.

We went straight back to the apartment, picked up Royal from *Babcia,* and after she fussed at me I went upstairs to my place. I dropped my purse on the floor, went directly to the bathroom, took a shower, and climbed into bed and Joseph's waiting arms.

He held me all night long and I didn't even try to sleep. Because every time I closed my eyes all I saw was Alicia's bloated face, and milky eyes, staring up at the sky.

I was thankful when it was time to go in to the office, thinking it would be best to stay busy. I dressed in comfortable and comforting clothes, my boyfriend jeans, and a ribbed navy sweater. I looped a fringed infinity scarf around my neck and slipped on my camel colored, low heeled boots. Royal ended up coming along with me—I certainly wasn't going to leave him and the cat alone in my apartment together. Who knows what they'd get into, or tear up.

On the drive in, Royal sat in the passenger seat with his nose pressed against the cracked car window, sniffing the breeze.

"What am I going to do with you now?" I wondered.

Royal looked back at me with a canine grin. He had a new bedazzled leash attached to his collar, courtesy of my sister Vanessa. According to *Babcia,* my sister had run out and picked up dog food and a leash yesterday. "I should probably take you home to Franklin."

The dog growled in response.

"What's the matter Royal?" I asked. "Don't you like Franklin?"

With a little whine, Royal turned around and nudged me. I gave him an absent pat on the head and was rewarded with a doggy kiss.

"Euww." I wiped the dog slobber off my hand and kept driving.

I unlocked the office door, letting myself in the back of Beth's house as was my habit. Royal followed neatly at my heels like a little pug shadow. Pulling a chair over by my desk, I patted the cushioned seat, and Royal hopped right up. I unhooked his leash, he circled once, wagged his curled tail, and was snoring away in a few moments.

"You sleep more than Squash does." I shook my head over the dog and began working my way through the files on my desk. I tried to anyway, but kept reading the same client file over and over. I heard Beth coming down the steps from the second floor and towards our offices that she'd created on the first floor of the house.

The phone rang, and I waved at her in greeting as she walked in. "Good Morning," I said with false cheer into the phone. "Danvers Paranormal Investigations. How can I help you?"

"Is this Nilah Stefanik?" a voice inquired.

"Yes, this is Nilah, can I help you?"

"This is Larry Paulson, from the Danvers Sentinel. I understand that you claim to be some type of medium. Is that how you found the body of Mrs. Fogg?"

"No comment," I said, quickly hanging up. "That was a reporter," I explained to Beth.

"The phone calls from the press started at five o'clock this morning," Beth said softly.

"What?" I blinked at her. "How did they know to call here?"

"One of the reporters at the scene recognized me from a Halloween interview about local haunted locations," Beth admitted. "Even though I didn't speak to him yesterday, he must have done some digging, and found out that you worked here."

"There were reporters at the police station, when Joseph and I left as well." I shook my head at the realization that I had been identified to the press. "I suppose word got out. Damn it."

"People in town still talk about how you helped find my grandmother's stolen jewelry last year," Beth said. "That's partially my fault. My family was so determined to help you keep your job at the funeral home that we didn't stop and consider that telling our story—how you and Granny's ghost solved the mystery—could potentially make trouble for you."

The phone rang again and even though my hands were shaking, I made myself answer it. "Danvers Paranormal Investigations. How can I help you?"

"This is news channel 17 calling. We'd like to arrange an interview with Nilah Stefanik—"

I immediately hung up. "Another one," I told Beth.

Beth rested her hand on my shoulder. "It's going to be alright." The ringing of our business phone punctuated her words. "Let it go to voicemail," she suggested.

Before we could decide what to do next, the back door opened up and a gorgeous woman strolled right in. "Hello paranormal team!" she began, sounding all perky and cheerful. She was followed by a cameraman.

"This is private property!" Beth threw out her arms to block the woman. "You can't simply walk in."

I saw the cameraman hand her a microphone and begin to film. *This can't be happening,* I thought.

"Miss Stefanik, how do you feel about the possibility of Franklin Fogg being charged for the murder of his wife?" The reporter asked, swinging her microphone my way.

"*What*?" I stood up so fast that my rolling chair bounced off the wall behind me.

"Have you assisted the police department with murder investigations in the past?" She fired off.

"No comment!" I tried to sound firm.

Royal popped up, swung his head in the direction of the television crew, and started to growl. The television reporter continued to ask questions over Beth's warnings to leave, and with a loud bark, Royal leapt off the chair. In a blur of fawn and black colored fur, he went straight for the ankles of the television crew.

The female reporter shrieked and ducked behind the cameraman, but he wasn't quick enough to evade. Royal latched on to the hem of the man's jeans and was growling and shaking his head for all he was worth.

"Call him off!" the cameraman yelled.

I wasn't sure what command to use to get him to let go. "Stop! Release!" I shouted and Royal immediately let go of the man's pant's leg. "Heel," I said, snapping my fingers, and the pug trotted over. The dog stood, quivering beside me, and let out a little warning growl towards the television crew.

It sent them scrambling off the back porch faster than was dignified.

"And stay out!" Beth yelled as she slammed the door after them.

"Oh my god!" I suddenly wanted to laugh and cry all at the same time.

Beth flipped the lock on the door. "Where on

earth did that dog come from?"

I couldn't help it. I started to laugh. Royal tipped his head up, met my eyes, and his tongue rolled out. "You." I bent over to scrub his black ears. "Are way too smart for your own good."

Royal gave a quick bark, turned in a circle, and sat.

"I didn't know you had a dog." Beth crouched down and held out her hand for Royal to sniff.

"I don't," I said, as Royal darted over to her. "I'm watching him for a while until I can find him a new home."

"What, your fostering a rescue dog?" Beth chuckled as Royal began to go through a series of tricks. He offered a paw and then rolled over.

"No, he's not a rescue. This is Royal, he was Alicia's dog."

Beth's eyes were round in her face. "How did *you* end up with him?"

"He sort of showed up on my porch yesterday." I shrugged. "Alicia said she sent the dog to me. She was worried about him."

Beth scooped the sturdy pug up and held him in her arms. She laughed as the dog began licking her face. "I remember reading in the paper that her dog had won some best in show prize at an important competition. Last year, I think it was."

"She said he was a champion." I sucked in a quick breath as an awful thought occurred to me. "You don't think somebody killed Alicia to take her dog out of competition, do you?"

"I don't know." Beth blew her bangs out of her eyes. "I mean, it's not any crazier than hearing Franklin Fogg could be a suspect in his wife's death."

Royal began to whine and he laid his head on Beth's shoulder.

"I think we'd better call Rick," Beth said.

I sighed. "I didn't mention the dog during all the questioning yesterday. It hadn't seemed important, but that detective—Tucker, was his name—he did tell me to contact him if I had *any* other information."

"We should call them both," Beth agreed and gave Royal a kiss on the head. "Don't you worry," she said to the dog. "We won't let anyone get you."

***

By the time Detective Tucker and Rick arrived, they had to wade through several reporters. Rick was only too happy to inform them that they were not allowed on the property so they all moved their vans from the back driveway to out front on the street.

While they couldn't come up to the door anymore, they could still hover at the curb and watch for us to leave. Which really didn't make me feel any better knowing they were out there waiting to pounce.

I explained to the detective how Royal had showed up on my doorstep, and the older man didn't react much. He did contact Franklin Fogg, Alicia's husband, and ask if he'd like his dog returned to him. I watched the detective's face when Franklin informed him that he wanted nothing to do with the dog.

The detective ended his call and gave me a cool stare. "Well, that was interesting."

"I could hear Franklin over the phone," I said. "He sounded sort of angry about Royal." I glanced down at the dog who was asleep on the floor next to my chair.

"Ms. Stefanik, how well do you know Mr. Fogg?" Detective Tucker asked coolly.

"I told you yesterday," I reminded him. "I worked at the Fogg Funeral home offices for a few months last year. Franklin was always very kind to me—"

"Right up until he fired you," Detective Tucker said.

"Technically it was his wife who fired me."

"And did you resent her for that?"

"No detective, I didn't hold any grudges against the woman." I sat back in my chair and smiled over at Beth and Rick who sat on the opposite side of my desk. "I'm very happy with my job here managing the office at DPI."

"Do they pay you to consult as a medium on haunted house cases?" His question was so smooth and unexpected that I hadn't realized he'd switched gears on me.

"No, of course not," I said.

"*Do* you consult?"

"Sometimes."

The detective ran a hand through his salt and pepper hair. "I'll be honest with you Ms.

Stefanik. I don't believe in mediums or psychics."

"I understand." I gave him a slight smile, trying to put the man at ease.

He frowned. "I don't believe in *any* of this; haunted houses, ghosts, fortune tellers, or Gypsy curses..."

I started to laugh. "You'll have to meet my grandmother sometime."

There was a sharp rapping sound on the back door. My *babcia* was standing on the back porch, and she appeared none-too-pleased.

"Speak of the devil," Detective Tucker muttered.

I hurried to unlock the door. My grandmother swept in wearing a flowing black dress and a colorful fringed shawl in turquoise wrapped around her shoulders. She was still a striking woman in her seventies, and I hoped to look half as good as she did when I reached that age.

Although the Detective had said he didn't believe in psychics, the older man still rose to his feet immediately when my grandmother entered the room.

"*Wnucka*." My grandmother pressed a kiss to

my cheek. "I felt the need to check on you. The reporters, they have been a nuisance at the shop all morning."

"I'm sorry, *Babcia*."

"Bah!" She waved my apology away, and bracelets in every metal imaginable clanged merrily on her wrists. "I can handle a bunch of nosey reporters." She suddenly spotted the detective. "Who do we have here?"

"This is Detective Tucker," I introduced him. "Detective, this is my grandmother, Sabina Abrams."

"You are helping my *wnucka*— granddaughter, yes?"

"Ma'am." The detective held out his hand to my grandmother.

"Detective Tucker says he doesn't believe in psychics, mediums...or Gypsy curses," I couldn't resist adding.

"No offense," Detective Tucker said, glancing from me to my grandmother.

"Professionally, I am called Madame Sabina." She grasped his offered hand. "But you may call me Sabina." She smiled, and tugged the detective a tad closer. "And to be clear, I do not deal in curses."

A flush rode up the detective's neck. "Er..." he stammered. "That's good to know."

"Ah yes." Her eyes narrowed as she studied the detective. "You are Dennis."

"That's right," Detective Tucker said, smiling politely. Then he did a double take. "I never told you my first name."

My grandmother smiled slowly and directly into his eyes. "No, you did not."

CHAPTER SIX

The detective pulled his hand away. "You're very good. You almost had me there for a moment."

My grandmother raised her brows. "Dennis, you must know that my Nilah is a good girl. She is not an attention seeker, and never would she harm another person."

"Ma'am," the detective began, "this nonsense about your granddaughter saying that the spirit of Alicia James-Fogg led her to the body, has resulted in her becoming a person of interest in our investigation."

"*Nonsense*!" My grandmother scowled. "And why do you find the idea so very hard to believe?" my grandmother asked.

"Because people can't speak to the dead," he

said patiently.

Rick gave up his chair for my grandmother and with a gracious nod, she took her seat. "Detective," she said. "I see that you are a good man."

"Well, thank you," he replied, sounding a little confused.

My grandmother smiled. "So I will not hold your narrow-mindedness against you."

"*Babcia,*" I cautioned her. "He's only doing his job."

"And when you look at the detective Nilah, who do you see around him?"

Her question caught me off guard. She'd never asked such a thing before. I turned my head, studied the detective. There was a feminine presence around him. *His mother*, I realized. *His mother's spirit was staying close to her son.* I couldn't see her, but I suddenly felt her, and unbidden, personal information about the detective popped unexpectedly into my mind—and right out of my mouth.

"Your mother called you Denny Dee when you were little." I heard myself say.

Detective Tucker flinched. "Good god."

"She made peach preserves from an old tree that grew in her backyard, every summer until..." I trailed off when it hit me why she'd stopped. "Until this summer, because she passed away in May."

The detective froze in place. "There's no way on earth that you could know that."

Her laughter wrapped around me, and I felt a very real, warm, and loving presence. I began to smile in reaction as she relayed even more information.

Tell him, his mother's spirit whispered in my mind.

"She says to remind you of when you fell out of that old peach tree. It was in the summertime, you were ten and the fall broke your arm." I tried to stop, but the information kept coming. "You have a new granddaughter," I said. "And your son named her after his grandmother." I felt tears well up. "He named her Anya...Your mother is pleased as punch about that, by the way."

"She always said that..." The detective stared at me with very large eyes. "*Pleased as punch.*"

As quick as it had begun, the flow of

information stopped, and Anya was gone. "Whoa." A sharp headache stabbed behind my eyes. I shook my head, and the room spun around me.

"Nilah." Rick grabbed my arm and gave it a little squeeze. "Hey! Are you okay?"

"Wow." I huffed out a breath, awed by what had happened. "That was new."

"Your eyes," Beth said, "they changed. Your pupils were huge when you were 'reading' the detective."

"I *knew* it." My grandmother nodded her head. "Didn't I tell you, your abilities would expand and grow?"

I shifted my attention to the detective, and his face was set in stern lines. "I'm sorry if I upset you Detective Tucker. That wasn't planned."

He stayed where he was, studying me intently. "I'm a trained observer, Ms. Stefanik. You are shaking and noticeably paler. I can see that sharing this information wasn't easy on you."

"There is always a physical cost when speaking with the dead." My grandmother's voice was quiet but firm.

"Which is why I don't particularly enjoy doing it." I accepted the cup of water Rick pushed on me and took a sip.

"Is that the reason you don't do readings at your grandmother's psychic parlor?" the detective asked.

"It's one of them," I said.

"Your sister does readings." The detective folded his arms. "I've checked into it."

"I am *not* a psychic," I tried to explain. "I have very little talent for public tarot readings."

He frowned. "You're not..." he trailed off and tried again "You mean to say that you *don't* see the future?"

"No, I never have."

"Not all psychics see the future?" The detective seemed genuinely curious now.

"No, they do not," my grandmother cut in. "A true psychic-clairvoyant would see the future, the present *and* the past. A medium communicates with the dead, and they may or may not be a psychic."

"Basically, I'm like a messenger." I tried to help the detective understand. "A sort of go-between that interprets messages to living people from the spirits on the other side."

"Detective Dennis," my grandmother said. "You can take me to lunch now that your shift is over, and I will explain the differences of psychic abilities to you over a meal." She stood, reached into her purse and handed me a little bottle of aspirin. "Here, this will help with the headache."

I accepted the bottle gratefully. "*Dziękuję*— thank you," I said.

Babcia patted my cheek. She turned, slipped her hand in the crook of Detective Tucker's arm, and steered him towards the exit. As he opened the door for her, she tossed me a wink and then gave her full attention to the detective.

Rick shut and locked the door behind them. He came back with a rueful smile on his face. "That was one of the smoothest shuffles I've ever seen."

"That's my *babcia*." I smiled in agreement. "I hope she takes it easy on him."

"Dennis has been divorced for five years," Rick said. "It will do him good to spend some time with her."

Beth was staring like she'd never seen me before. "What you just did?" she said. "That was impressive, Nilah."

"I wasn't trying to impress anyone." I shrugged.

"I know." She smiled. "That's what made it all the more remarkable."

***

We were unusually busy at DPI that day. Suddenly everyone in town was convinced their house was haunted. Vanessa called me from the shop to inform me that the psychic parlor had over a dozen walk-ins, all wanting a medium style reading—from me.

"One woman offered to pay you five hundred dollars," Vanessa chuckled.

"Are you kidding me?"

"No I'm not," she said. "How's Royal doing today?"

I eyeballed the dog. He was napping beside my desk, his head resting on a mangled, yellow ball. "Beth gave him an old tennis ball earlier. He went a little insane chasing it around the back yard with her." I rolled my eyes as the pug snored away. "Right now he's crashed."

"Pugs sleep a lot," Vanessa said. "I wanted to check in. I had the weirdest little flash that he'd been in trouble. I kept thinking he'd torn up a pair of blue jeans."

"He tussled with a news crew this morning," I admitted. "The cameraman had been wearing jeans. Royal went after him and when they wouldn't leave, he gave his cuff a good shake."

Vanessa burst out laughing. "Ah, well that explains the vision. We've been dealing with reporters as well, they've been asking some pretty rude questions."

"Is it bad?"

"I know you aren't comfortable with questions about your mediumship abilities. And you kept a pretty low profile after the jewelry incident last year. But, you need to brace yourself, Nilah. The cat is out of the bag. People are not going to let this go."

"Okay." I rubbed my forehead and reached for the aspirin bottle.

"Don't be surprised if you have to dodge a few reporters when you come home," Vanessa warned.

"Terrific," I sighed.

"Nilah, please be careful," Vanessa urged.

Caught off guard by the sincere words and genuine concern in her tone, I faltered. "Ah yeah. Sure. Why wouldn't I be?" I purposefully changed the subject. "How's my niece?"

"Vanda tried to take a few steps yesterday," Vanessa announced.

"She did?" I laughed and felt some of the tension ease up. "Obviously the girl's a prodigy," I said, knowing it would please my sister.

"Love you," Vanessa said, and hung up.

I stared at the receiver. I couldn't recall the last time she'd said that to me. I shrugged it off, maybe it was simply a side-effect of all that had happened in the past few days. *More reporters waiting for me when I came home?* I groaned and took a few more aspirin.

***

There were three of them.

The reporters had arranged themselves along

the back parking area behind the shop. I pulled my car in, snagged my purse and took a firm hold of Royal's sparkly leash. "Here we go," I muttered, climbing out of the car. Royal hopped out right behind me.

"Ms. Stefanik!" a man shouted. "Is it true that you think you're a medium?"

"Are you consulting on cases with the Danvers Police Department now?" a second one asked.

I shut my car door, ignored them and made my way to the back gate.

"Are you doing all this for attention?" a third voice asked.

I hesitated, inwardly cringing at the question. *Do not turn around.* I reminded myself. I shoved the gate open, Royal dashed inside the back patio area, and I let the gate slam behind me. I thought the reporters wouldn't come onto our patio if I ignored them, and I was mistaken.

I'd taken two steps when a hand fell on my shoulder. "Do you know who killed Alicia James-Fogg?" The leering male reporter was standing way too close.

"Back off." I yanked away from him, and

suddenly, a spray of water shot across the back patio, splattering my assailant in the face.

"Get out!" My sister Vanessa shouted.

I swung my head around at her voice and stood staring. On the brick patio my stunning little sister stood, armed with the garden hose my grandmother used to water her planters and containers.

"You can't come back here!" Vanessa yelled, taking aim at another reporter. With Vanda perched on her hip, she expertly sprayed the man down with water.

"Hey!" the reporter tossed his arms up to shield himself from the spray.

I couldn't help but laugh at the craziness of the situation. While Vanessa hosed all the intruders down, I tugged the dog farther back and hurried away from the reporters who were frantically trying to cover up their cameras and phones. "Stand down, warrior princess," I said, making my way to her side.

Royal barked and spun in a circle. Excited by all the commotion, the baby bounced and squealed in delight.

"*Śmieć*!"Vanessa shouted, sending a final arc

of water their way. It nailed one of the reporters in the butt, and the annoying trio went scurrying. Vanessa bent and shut the water off with one fast movement. "Quick, come inside," she urged.

I ducked in the back door of the shop and stood staring at my sister, while the dog barked and the baby clapped. "Are you insane?" I asked her.

"Nobody fucks with my family," she growled.

My eyes almost bugged out of my head. "You dropped the F bomb in front of the baby."

"She's too young to understand." Vanessa tossed a long cable of golden brown hair over her shoulder. "They've been hanging around the shop asking the most obnoxious questions and I've had enough."

"Clearly." I eyeballed my little sister and wondered what had gotten into her.

"I couldn't even take the baby to the car without them swarming us. *Śmieć*," she said again—the Polish word for trash.

All because of me, I realized. "Vanessa," I began, "I'm really sorry."

She shrugged. "I suppose I better wait a while before I try and take the baby home."

"You could come upstairs. Have dinner with us while you wait for them to leave," I offered impulsively, not expecting her to take me up on it.

"Perfect," she said, and had me blinking in surprise. Vanessa picked up the baby's bag and her purse. "Let's take the interior stairs up to your place."

Joseph came home a half-hour later to Vanessa and me working side-by-side in the kitchen, while Vanda sat on a quilt in the middle of the living room rug. Squash had retreated to the safety of the top of the refrigerator, and my brown eyed niece was laughing at the dog. Royal seemed to think it was a great game to prance over to the baby, yip, and then bounce backwards. Every time he did, my niece would squeal and let loose with a gut-busting laugh.

Joseph grinned at the baby, but did a double take at me and my sister together. "How lucky am I to come home to three beautiful girls?" he said smoothly. The baby took one glance at

Joseph and tossed her arms up in the air. Joseph scooped her up from the ground and rubbed his beard against the baby's neck, sending her into more shrieks of delight.

Between the dog yapping, the baby squealing, and Squash meowing his disapproval of the ruckus in his normally quiet abode, it was happy chaos.

Vanessa and Vanda stayed with us for a few hours after dinner. Later, when Joseph walked my sister and niece to their car, he said there were no reporters. I was relieved to hear it and hoped they wouldn't come back. We climbed into bed and Squash claimed his spot at my side. The dog wouldn't come into the bedroom with the cat holding court, and exhausted, I fell into a deep sleep.

CHAPTER SEVEN

It was the whining that woke me. Disoriented, I opened my bleary eyes to find Royal springing up and down at the side of the bed. "Jeez, Royal." I gave him a half-hearted pat on the head and scooted over closer to Joseph.

The dog managed to make the jump to the mattress and landed beside me. Squash began to yowl at the invasion and the dog growled, holding his space. I rolled over, ready to boot the pair of them off the bed when Royal charged the cat with some fairly impressive barking.

"What the hell?" Joseph sat up.

Squash retreated, and Royal started going bat shit. He let out a little yip and grabbed my hand in his mouth. He didn't bite down, but he tugged.

"What in the world has gotten into you?" I asked the dog crossly. Then the alarms starting going off.

"That's the carbon monoxide alarm!" Joseph sprang out of bed and tossed on a pair of jeans.

"*Babcia*!" I said. "We have to get her out of the building." I jumped up, and could suddenly smell sulfur. I tossed on a robe, slipped my cell phone in my pocket and Joseph quickly pulled Squash's cat carrier out of the closet. I nabbed the cat, earning myself a few scratches while I shoved him in the carrier.

The dog kept barking the entire time.

Joseph picked up the pug and tucked Royal under his arm like a furry football. He grabbed my hand and together we rushed to the door, away from the carbon monoxide and to the fresh air outside. Babcia met us on her landing with her cats already in their carrier, and we all hurried down the steps and out to the back courtyard.

Joseph passed the dog to me as he called the fire department. Royal whined and licked my chin. "You're a good boy," I said, burying my face against his fur.

"I heard the alarm going off. But the dog, he woke you up *before* the alarm, didn't he?" My grandmother stood with her arms crossed over her chest.

"He did." I gave the beastie a kiss on top of his homely head.

My grandmother scratched Royal under his chin. "You are a hero," she said. "I'm going to buy you a steak."

Royal began to bark excitedly, recognizing the word *steak*. I rolled my eyes at the dog, and waited with my grandmother. In the distance, sirens wailed and the cats joined in, yowling unhappily in their carriers.

The official word was that the main line on the outside of our building was old and faulty which was more than a little alarming. Once the gas was shut off, the line would have to be repaired. In the meantime the building had to air out, and it was suggested that we wait a few days to return to our apartments and to re-open the shop.

In the interim, concerned neighbors and

clients called. My parents fussed over my grandmother, and the menagerie and I stayed with Joseph. I was called back to the police department for a follow up interview two days after the gas leak.

It was actually a fairly polite interrogation. I was informed that the time of death for Alicia had been established, and the detective wanted to know my whereabouts. Fortunately for me, I had an alibi. I'd actually been at work at DPI with Beth at the office all day, and since Joseph had worked late that night, Rick had taken me and Beth out for pizza. Call that corroborated alibi serendipity, good luck, or magick, I didn't care. I was relieved when they let me leave.

Alicia's family had been all over the news. They'd interviewed her brother and parents, who seemed to be standing by Franklin, and the rumor mill around town was pretty intense. Everyone had an opinion, or a theory. I kept my mouth shut and made a herculean effort to avoid the evening news or the newspapers.

I'd worked a shorter shift at DPI as Beth had a paranormal investigation scheduled for the evening. After work I'd gone back to Joseph's house thinking I could unwind. But instead, I ended up having a front row seat to a challenge for dominance between the cat and the dog.

Squash was having a great time punking Royal. The cat would sneak over and dive bomb the snoozing dog, and Royal would jump up and tear around the house chasing the cat in retaliation. The two of them seemed to think it was a great game, but I was going a little stir crazy.

My sexy man-beast wasn't due home for another hour, and in the past few moments the barking and chasing was getting a little too frantic for my comfort. Clearly my idea of letting Royal and Squash hash it out for themselves was a no-go. So I decided to leash up Royal and take him for a walk.

I tossed on a lined leather jacket over my black leggings and long denim shirt, determined to have a little quiet time, and maybe even enjoy the last of the autumn leaves as they fell. As I locked up, I saw that Squash had plopped himself in the middle of the coffee table.

"Meow," he cried, smugly.

"You're kind of a jerk, Squash," I chastised as I left. Squash obviously wasn't fazed. He ignored me and continued to clean his paws.

As Royal and I walked down the sidewalk, all skirmishes appeared forgotten. The dog was practically prancing on his leash. He held his head high and was very well behaved as we traveled towards the local park. A chilly breeze was stripping away any remaining leaves from the trees, and I shivered in my jacket. After a quick walk through the park, I picked up the pace on the trip home, hoping it would warm me up.

A jogger was making his way down the sidewalk towards us. I had a moment to sum him up as a serious runner, and affluent. He was trim, jogging at an easy pace, and outfitted in top of the line, coordinated running gear. As he started to approach on our left, Royal lunged forward, barking furiously at the man.

"Royal, no!" I yanked on his leash, but the pug was determined. "Bad dog!" I said, as he pulled me down the sidewalk and squared off with the jogger.

The man broke stride and came to a halt.

"Stupid dog," he swore, and pushed his wrap-around sunglasses to the top of his head.

With a jolt of shock, I recognized the runner. It was Franklin Fogg, Alicia's husband. "Franklin, what are you doing out here?"

He focused on me. "I was out for a run," he said.

"Well, yes, I can see that," I said, tugging Royal back away from him. "I meant, why are you running in *this* neighborhood? You live clear across town."

"Not that it's any of your business." Franklin seemed barely out of breath. "I sometimes jog through, and around, the local park."

I yanked the agitated pug back towards me. "Oh. I see."

"The park does have a 5-K trail." Franklin gave me a pointed look. "Not that you'd know."

I frowned over the snide comment, even as the dog continued to bark. "Royal, knock it off!" I said, tightening the leash. "Behave," I told the dog, pushing on his rump.

Royal relented with a whine and sat. On my tennis shoes.

"I suppose you're proud of yourself.

Managing to get your name in the papers again," Franklin said.

"*What*?" I'd been about to offer my condolences, but now, I frowned at him.

"Still craving attention?"

"What are you talking about?"

"You. Speaking to reporters. Claiming to be a medium, and saying that Alicia's ghost led you to find her body." Franklin sneered. "And to think I once defended you."

"I never spoke to any reporters." It was the only reply I could think of.

Franklin scoffed and rolled his eyes.

"I didn't," I insisted, shocked at his attitude. I'd once thought him to be sympathetic and caring. But the person who stood before me barely resembled the kind man I'd once worked for.

"Do you have any idea of what I've been through in the past week?" He pointed an accusatory finger at me. "First the idiotic police questioning me about Alicia's death, and the absolute insanity of the media? Thank god I have a competent lawyer."

At a loss for words, I stood there and stared.

Franklin smoothed his hair back. "It's bad enough that I'm having to deal with her funeral in a few days...but now my name and reputation are also being impugned."

"Well, it's clearly obvious which part has you the most upset," I snarked. *My god,* I thought. *He was every bit as self-important and unfeeling as Alicia was.*

He puffed up. "The Fogg family had an impeccable reputation, until you managed to get yourself involved in Alicia's unfortunate demise and turned it all into a freak show!"

"Unfortunate demise?" I flipped his words back on him. "Yeah, that's some tough luck pal. Your wife inconveniently dying and having the nerve to tarnish your lofty family status and all."

He drew himself up. "You would never understand what a man in my position has been through. For the love of god, stay away from the funeral home," he ordered. "The last thing I need is a bigger media circus than I have now."

"Aw, really?" I pouted as if disappointed. "I was thinking I might make a nice, cheesy noodle casserole and bring it to your office."

"You little bitch."

"What, you don't do carbs?" I fluttered at him. "I could always send a big floral arrangement filled with neon green gladiolas. You know, something low key, classy and tasteful..."

He started to move forward, but the dog began to growl. It was low and mean, and Franklin stepped quickly back. "Stay away from the funeral," he said, dropping his shades back over his eyes. "Consider yourself warned." With that, he jogged to the opposite side of the street.

"What an asshole," I said to the dog. A cold breeze curled down my neck and I shivered. "Let's go home, Royal," I said. We walked on, but I kept replaying the conversation in my mind, and the more I thought about it, the more uneasy I became.

I would never have thought Franklin Fogg capable of violence...but now, after this, I wasn't so sure. "Don't play Nancy Drew, Nilah," I muttered. As I approached the street corner I tossed a quick glance over my shoulder, but saw no sign of Franklin.

"Where'd he go?" I squinted down in the direction I'd last seen him and jumped when the cell phone in my pocket began to ring. Checking the screen I saw that it was my sister calling. I pressed 'accept'. "Hey Vanessa."

"I dropped by Joseph's to check on you," she said. "Where are you?"

"I took Royal for a walk up to the park. I'm a couple of blocks over." I paused at the intersection while Royal sniffed the recycle bins at the curb. "We're heading back, actually."

"Good." Her voice was clipped. "Nilah you *should* come back."

I felt the nape of my neck prickle. "Is something wrong?"

"Come back to the house. Right now."

I rolled my eyes at my younger sister's bossiness, but gave the dog's leash a little tug. "Come on Royal." The dog heeled neatly. "Okay," I said into the phone. "We're on our way. Is everyone alright?"

"Yes. I'll meet you." Vanessa's voice sounded funny, and I could hear her jewelry jangling.

I smiled in the phone, and got a mental image of my fashionista sister running in heels. "Vanessa, are you *jogging*?"

"Yeah, and I'm carrying the baby," she huffed into the phone. "What street are you on right now?"

"I'm on Chestnut. What's the rush?"

"I have a terrible feeling..."

I stopped dead on the sidewalk. "As in a premonition?" I was about to press her for more information but Royal suddenly lunged forward on his leash. He bolted off the sidewalk into a grassy front yard to my left, and the leash strap around my wrist yanked me forward.

Catching movement out of the corner of my eye, I threw myself even further into the yard. A vehicle had jumped the curb from behind, and there was a terrible racket as the car hit the large recycle bins on the curb. They went bouncing past me with only the barest of grazes, and before I could blink, the car had careened back onto the street and disappeared around the corner.

"Nilah!" I heard Vanessa's shout from down the block.

I sat up on the grass. "*Dupek*!" I shouted after the driver. "Probably texting and driving." I shook my head at the driver's carelessness.

Royal jumped on me and began licking my face excitedly. "Thanks, Royal," I said, patting the dog.

Vanessa raced over. "Are you alright?"

"I'm fine." I took a quick mental inventory and counted myself lucky. I picked up my phone and rolled to my feet. As soon as I stood, Vanessa started brushing me off.

"You've got grass stains on your clothes," she fussed.

"It'll wash out," I said, as Royal began to jump against my sister's legs.

Vanda squealed from the excitement and reached out for me. I swung the baby to my hip, while my sister panted.

"Oh my god, oh my god!" Vanessa bent at the waist trying to catch her breath.

"I'm fine, Vanessa." I patted her back while she wheezed.

A front door opened, and a woman poked her head out. "Are you alright dear?" She surveyed us standing in her yard and stepped outside on her porch.

"Yes Ma'am." I tried to send her a reassuring smile. "Thanks, though."

"That blue SUV almost hit you," she said, coming down her porch steps. "I'm calling the police."

"I'm fine," I insisted. "It's okay."

Vanessa straightened up. "We need to get you back to Joseph's house."

"Now, let's not overreact," I cautioned. "It was probably some idiot texting while driving. The bins took a hit, but they didn't touch me."

"That wasn't an accident!" Vanessa insisted over Royal's excited barks. "I saw the whole thing!"

The concerned woman started speaking into her cell phone—calling the police, I presumed.

Royal's barking grew louder and more frantic. He circled us, wrapping his leash around our legs. Baby Vanda giggled and squealed at the dog's barking, and a few other neighbors came out to see what all the hubbub was about. Meanwhile, I tried to reassure Vanessa, hold on to an excited baby, and get us all untangled at the same time.

I yanked on the leash. "Royal! Stop. Sit!"

"Don't you yell at him!" Vanessa snapped, and burst into tears.

"Damn it!" I managed, but before I could do anything else—my sister made a funny little sound, and promptly fainted.

CHAPTER EIGHT

I was getting mighty damn tired of the fire department, paramedics, *and* police officers. When Vanessa's eyes had rolled back in her head I'd managed to make a grab for her, and between me and the nice neighbor lady, we'd let her slide to the ground.

Now all four of us—that four being me, the baby, my sister and the dog—were riding in an ambulance on the way to the hospital. My sister was currently on the stretcher holding ten-month old Vanda, and I sat next to them and off to the side. Royal had managed to charm the EMTs. He was riding shotgun in the front with the driver, with his doggy head sticking happily out of the passenger window.

No doubt about it. That dog has mad people

skills.

I had to call Joseph and tell him what had happened. I also asked him to contact my parents and Vanessa's husband. It wasn't a pleasant phone call.

When we arrived at the emergency room they whisked Vanessa off, and I was left walking the waiting room floor with my niece who had clearly had enough excitement for the day—and was wailing the walls down.

Twenty minutes later she'd cried herself to sleep on my shoulder. I kept walking with her anyway and noticed a large group of people right outside the doors. I braced myself as my brother-in-law, parents, two brothers, grandmother, *and* my lover burst through the ER doors at the same time.

They created quite the ruckus, and I wondered how long it would be before someone called security. My mother and brother-in-law, Tony, immediately began grilling the front desk nurse. My father tried to walk straight back to the treatment areas, and my brothers were arguing about who should go back to see Vanessa and who should stay with my grandmother.

Joseph was silent. He stalked straight over to me, and the set expression on his face had me holding out a preemptive hand.

"Before you yell," I began. "Remember that I'm holding a baby—"

Which didn't slow him down in the least. With a growl he scooped me straight up off the floor, baby and all, and laid one on me. Vanda slept right through it. When Joseph had finally lifted his lips from mine, I found myself hot, bothered, and a little out of breath.

"I swear to god, woman." Joseph laid his forehead against mine. "I'm not letting you out of my sight any time soon."

"I was taking Royal for a walk and all hell broke loose," I said quietly over Vanda's curls.

"Tell me what happened," my *babcia* demanded.

While Tony was ushered back to sit with his wife, I took a deep breath and explained to my family how we'd come to be at the hospital.

"Vanessa ran two blocks hauling the baby?" Nicolas asked.

Vincent, my older brother, smirked. "No

wonder she passed out."

My mother, Nadia, eased the baby out of my arms. "You must be more careful Nilah. More thoughtful about personal safety."

"I didn't do anything wrong," I said.

My mother cut me off with a stare that had me cringing. "We will talk later," she promised.

Feeling embarrassed by everyone's reaction, I sat back on the couch in the waiting room, shut my mouth, and held Joseph's hand.

A short time later Tony came out to talk to us. He was a little green around the gills himself as he announced that Vanessa was doing fine and they'd be releasing her shortly. Turns out that the reason she fainted was because she was pregnant. Again. And while the news was a bit of a shock, my family was thrilled.

"Good grief." My mother pressed a kiss to the top of Vanda's head. "They'll be less than eighteen months apart."

My father chuckled. "We know all about that, don't we Nadia?"

I smiled at the happy news. My brother Nicolas and I were only fourteen months apart and had been pretty tight growing up. "Congratulations." I smiled at my brother-in-law.

"Brace yourself, Anthony," my *babcia* said. "It's going to be another girl, with a temper to match her mother's."

My father clapped Anthony on the back. "Here's hoping they won't cause as much trouble as Nilah and Vanessa do."

"Hey!" I frowned over that comment as the rest of my family burst into laughter.

***

A week later, and things were back to whatever passes for normal with my family. I was very happy to be in my own apartment again, even as I stood in the kitchen, sipping tea and facing off with *Babcia.*

"The funeral for the James-Fogg woman is today." My grandmother planted her hands on her hips. "You should go and pay your respects."

"With all the excitement of finding out that Vanessa and Tony had a new baby on the way, I forgot," I fibbed.

"You are a terrible liar," my grandmother said.

"Well, it would be awkward," I admitted, pulling the belt on my robe tighter. "As I've been banned from the funeral."

"What does that mean?"

"Let me explain," I gestured to my kitchen table. We took a seat and I told her about my run-in with Franklin.

"Do you think he's involved somehow with his wife's death?"

I rubbed my arms. "It makes me break out in goose bumps thinking about that."

"Have you told the nice detective about your conversation with Franklin?"

"What for? To tell him Franklin is a pompous ass?" I rolled my eyes. "I'll bet you the detective is very aware of that."

"Nilah." My grandmother shook her head.

"If it makes you feel any better, I did talk to Joseph about it when we left the emergency room the other night."

"Oh?" my grandmother smiled. "And what did he say?"

"He went all caveman on me, even though I told him he was being overprotective."

"You are stubborn. Like your grandfather was." *Babcia* stood and dropped a kiss on top of my head. "I'll be downstairs in the reading parlor if you need anything."

"Don't go burning up the phone lines to your boyfriend, the detective," I teased her.

My grandmother stopped and turned slowly. Her eyes were serious when they met mine. "How did you know I was going to call him about this? Did your intuition tell you?"

"Afraid not," I shrugged, trying to act nonchalant. "That was more of an educated guess."

Babcia narrowed her eyes. "I think Nilah, you have more psychic talents than any of us could have ever predicted."

She let herself out and I took my tea over to the couch. I sat next to Squash who was curled along the back, studying the street below. The cat didn't even react when Royal jumped up and made himself at home, resting his head on my thigh.

I sat the mug down on the coffee table and

leaned my head back. Squash nudged the back of my head and began to purr. I was exhausted. I hadn't slept very much over the last few nights—not that I was complaining.

Joseph hadn't been happy with me after I'd filled him in on my bumping into Franklin. He'd even made a sly remark about wearing me out before I went back home, so I'd be too tired to get into anymore trouble.

I had originally rolled my eyes at his comment, and that had earned me a slow, considering stare out of the side of his eyes. He'd remained quiet when we'd picked up the dog and had driven back to his house.

Joseph had shut the front door behind us, and I'd unclipped Royal's leash. The dog made a mad dash towards the kitchen and his food bowls. I'd been smiling, distracted by the dog's antics, until Joseph bent over, grabbed my hips, and stood; tossing me over his shoulder in one smooth motion.

I'd started to laugh—at first. "Hey, caveman!" I said, thumping my fist against his hip. "You made your point. I'm sorry you were worried."

His response was a low, rumbling growl and a playful smack to my butt. "You were warned." He hauled me up the stairs to his bedroom and dumped me on the bed where I landed with a bounce.

"Well, wasn't that suave?" I shoved my hair out of my eyes and glared. "I think your nickname has gone to your head."

"You think so?" He didn't smile, only began unbuttoning his heavy denim work shirt.

"Listen, it's been a hell of a—" Every coherent thought I had simply left me as he stripped off the shirt and tossed it aside.

He stood, bare to the waist, and shook his hair back. "You were saying?"

He knew what that did to me. My gut clenched, and I smiled up at him. "I can't honestly remember."

Deliberately, he crawled over the bed and then swooped in with a hard, sexy kiss. And Joseph did indeed 'wear me out' until I was too tired to think, move, or even argue. To my further delight he'd been particularly *focused* for the rest of the time I'd stayed with him as well, and it had been wonderful.

As I reminisced, a soft November rain began to splatter against the windows of my apartment. Cozy, warm, and very relaxed, I stretched out on my sofa and dozed off with a contented smile on my face...

I stood in the misty rain with Royal by my side. I huddled under a black umbrella and shivered as I stared down at an open grave. The dog was unusually quiet and I felt him press against my ankle for comfort.

I recognized the old cemetery, but was surprised to notice that I was alone. No other people were gathered around the grave, and the metal chairs arranged so neatly for family, were empty. Several large floral arrangements were stacked precisely along the graveside. But something was off.

The grave shouldn't be left open like this. Even in my dream I knew that was wrong.

"We're not finished," a familiar voice said.

Alicia James-Fogg stood next to me. Still in her stained and torn clothes. Her hair remained tangled around her face which was much too pale. In fact, she looked sort of gray.

"You're not wearing your fancy blue suit." It was the first thing that came to mind. "They didn't bury you in your suit from Paris?"

"No." She shook her head. "Not like I'd hoped."

"I'm sorry, Alicia," I said, as gently as possible.

"It didn't matter. No one saw me." Alicia sniffled. "It was a closed casket."

As we stood beside the open grave the rain began to fall harder. The pattering sound it made against my umbrella seemed unnaturally harsh.

"Franklin gave away all my clothes," Alicia complained. "To charity, if you can believe that."

"He did?"

She clamped a hand on my forearm and her grip felt icy. "He sold my jewelry too." Now her voice was angry. "He's obviously glad to be rid of me...and you must be more careful. That car didn't accidentally jump the curb. It was aiming for you."

Shocked at both her words and feeling physical contact, I glanced down. Her right hand seemed to burn straight through my leather jacket. "Alicia, let go," I gasped, struggling to break away from her.

"Listen to me!" she said leaning into my face. "He thinks you know!"

"What?" I asked. "Who thinks I know?"

"He thinks you know!" she repeated.

"You're hurting me!" I tried to yank free of her grip and the dog began to whine.

"I can only do so much to help you," Alicia insisted, while the pressure on my arm became painful. "Hit the books, you fool."

"Stop it!" I wrenched my arm loose, and Alicia stumbled. She fell silently backwards, and disappeared into the open grave.

The first thing I became aware of was that the dog *was* actually whining. I tried to shake myself out of the dream, and the ringtone of my cell phone had me jolting. I pulled it from my robe's pocket and answered automatically. "Hello?" I said, while my heart pounded.

"Nilah?"

"Beth?" I asked as adrenalin raced through me.

"Nilah, are you okay?"

I pressed a hand to my galloping heart. "What time is it?"

"It's 9:45," she said. "We wanted to check in on you. You were supposed to be here fifteen minutes ago."

I nudged Royal aside and staggered to my feet. "Oh shit. I'm sorry Beth. I must have dozed off."

She blew out an audible breath. "It's no biggie. But after all the weird stuff you've had going on lately, Rick and I wanted to make sure you were all right."

"I'm sorry you were worried." I apologized again and headed for the bathroom. "I'm up. I'm moving."

"Listen," Beth said. "Take your time."

The dream flashed in my mind, and shaken, I detoured, sinking into a nearby kitchen chair. "Hey Beth, would you mind if I came in at noon?" I went for a casual tone and pulled it off. "I'll stop and grab us some burgers and fries for lunch."

"You had me at fries."

I almost laughed. "Okay I'll see you at

noon."

"Sounds good," Beth replied. "And Nilah?"

"Yeah?"

"Keep your phone with you."

"Will do." I disconnected the call, dropped the cell back in my robe pocket and headed to the bathroom. Turning the water on cold, I stuck my hands under the flow and splashed water in my face. Reaching blindly for the towel I patted my face dry and tried to shake off the creepy images from the dream.

I slid the towel away from my face and my eyes caught the reflection of my hands and wrists in the mirror.

There was a purple discoloration peeking out from under the cuff on my right sleeve. With a gasp I dropped the towel and shoved the sleeve up to my elbow.

A perfect purple handprint was on my forearm. I rotated my arm and noticed that the thumbprint was clearly visible on the underside of my arm as well. My heart began to race again as Alicia's words played back through my mind.

"That car was aiming for you. He thinks you

know! Hit the books, you fool...."

Even though I didn't understand the paranormal forces at work, somehow in an effort to warn me, Alicia's spirit *had* managed to make physical contact while I'd been sleeping—and I had the bruises to prove it.

"My first psychic vision in a dream." I shuddered. "And it was a doozy." There was a time when I'd have been thrilled over that, but now my stomach gave a nasty pitch at the realization that I was in real danger. My first thought was to go to my grandmother, but I went back to the living room instead, heading for the old rustic hutch where I stored my books and a few other magickal accessories. Maybe I should, 'hit the books' as ordered...

What I saw had me stopping in my tracks. The cat was sitting on the hutch next to my books, and Royal was jumping up and down trying to get to the cat. "Knock it off you two," I said, trying to sound firm even as my voice quivered.

It wasn't the animals that had me spooked. All the books and accessories on the hutch had been reorganized—and not by me. My large crystal ball was now holding the pages open of a big, hard back tome. I eased closer and discovered that the book was one on dream interpretation. It had been a present from my friend Christy.

"Magick or paranormal activity?" I wondered, surveying the re-arrangement.

"Meow." Squash rested his paw on top of the open pages.

Carefully I moved the crystal ball to the side, and Squash climbed off the book. I sat in a nearby arm chair and started to flip through the pages. Royal waddled over and rested his head on my feet as I checked for the definitions of the main symbols of the graveyard 'dream'.

The book was arranged alphabetically. I flipped to G for graveyards, and graves. "Dreaming of an open grave," I read out loud. "Bad luck, suffering for the crimes of others, and danger surrounds you." I gulped, but tried to take it in stride.

Well, the definitions were hardly shocking considering everything. A little clap of thunder punctuated my words and had me jumping. I flipped to U and checked out the symbolism for umbrellas.

"The umbrella," I read, "represents sanctuary and shelter. It may, however, show a reluctance to deal with negative emotions or trauma. If the umbrella is open in your dream you are protecting yourself from things in your own subconscious." I kept reading. "An open umbrella in the rain is an omen of good luck and signifies shelter from scary situations or harsh elements."

Gently I closed the book and slid it back on the main part of the hutch. My mind raced as I considered my options. I obviously required both spiritual and physical protection of some sort—and I bet that Christy would have some witchy ideas on that front. I should definitely show the bruise to Beth and see what she had to say about Alicia's spirit communicating with me *and* making physical contact in a dream.

Also, I needed to confirm for myself that Alicia *had* indeed been buried. So welcome or not, I was going to swing by the cemetery today. Pulling the phone out of my pocket I took some pictures of the bruises on my arm.

I sent a text message to both Beth and

Christy: *Had a dream/vision. Alicia warned me of danger and grabbed my arm. When I woke up a bit ago I found this.*

I sent the pictures along with a request that they meet me at DPI headquarters at noon to discuss the situation.

Feeling a little more in control, I headed for my room and got dressed for the day.

CHAPTER NINE

Sitting in my car, I discreetly watched the graveside ceremony. Royal snoozed away on the passenger seat, and his snuffling sound was sort of comforting. It was 11:00 in the morning, and the day was gloomy, rainy and cold. The mourners were huddled under umbrellas and had to have been miserable in the rain. Even as I felt sympathy for them, I stayed where I was and watched them all from afar.

When the passenger door of my car was yanked open, I almost jumped through the roof. Royal snapped awake and his tail began to wag.

A striking woman wearing an iridescent black trench coat and jeans eased in next to me. "I knew I'd find you here."

"Christy!" I pressed my hands to my heart.

"You scared the crap out of me!"

She scooted the pug over and shut the door behind her. "Hanging around graveyards?" She arched an eyebrow. "Better watch that, folks will start to talk...Oh wait. They already are."

"Now I've got a real Witch in my car," I shot back. "That'll really give them something to gossip about."

"Hey, I tucked my pentagram." Christy shook the raindrops from her dark brown hair. "I'm practically incognito."

"Yeah the black, shimmery trench coat is very subtle. What are you doing here?" I asked.

"Checking on you." Her blue eyes were serious. "I didn't scroll through the messages on my phone until about a half hour ago. When I discovered the photos you sent, I wanted to see you immediately. And I thought to myself, where would Nilah be?"

Royal decided to introduce himself and leaned over into Christy's face. He sniffed her hair and simply stared at her with his head cocked over to one side.

"This is Royal," I said. "He's friendly."

"Hi pup." Christy smiled at the dog. "You

wanna hop in the back while I have a few words with your mistress?"

I sat openmouthed as Royal climbed between the seats and settled quietly in the back. "How did you get him to do that?"

"I'm sort of *tuned in* to animals," she said.

"Is that a Witch thing?" I asked.

"You might say that." Christy grinned for a moment, but then her expression became more serious. "Let me see your arm."

I pushed up the sleeve of my green pea coat and held out my arm to her. "What do you think?"

She ran her fingertips gently over the purple marks. "I've read about this phenomena, but I've never seen it in person." Christy held her hand up as a comparison. "The shape of the bruise is small...as if a woman's hand made the mark."

"I didn't do this to myself." I said.

"I know." Christy smirked at me. "The bruise is on your right forearm...and see?" She wrapped her right hand around my arm covering the marks. "The markings correspond to a right hand, including where the little bruise from the thumb falls."

I winced a bit when she pressed her thumb in. "Oh. Aren't you smart?"

"Someone or *something* else had to have done this...you couldn't have managed to mark yourself up like that." Christy slid her hand away. "Nilah, I believe you. More importantly, do you believe the warning that the spirit sent you?"

"That's why I'm here. I thought maybe I should stay and watch over the burial." I sighed. "It probably sounds stupid."

"Not at all," Christy said. "It makes sense to me that you'd want to see this through."

Out of the corner of my eye I saw people beginning to leave. "The graveside service is over."

"Check that out," Christy said as we watched the crowd. "Not one sad face among the mourners."

I scrutinized the expressions of the people who were heading towards nearby cars. "They look sort of annoyed, actually." I said, and the fact that they did made the hair rise on the back of my neck.

Christy let out a low whistle. "By the Goddess, no one even *liked* that woman."

"That's true," I agreed. "She was obnoxious. But still, no one deserves to die and be left in the woods the way she was."

"Tell you what," Christy said. "I'll follow you over to DPI, and let's have a sit down with Beth and see what the three of us can conjure up." She reached for the door handle. "It's going to be okay. We'll make it okay. Don't worry, Nilah."

I didn't have the chance to answer her. As soon as she opened the car door, Royal squeezed behind the car seat and made a break for it. "Shit!" I pushed open my door and went after him. "Royal, stop!"

My command was useless. The dog tore across the road and through the cemetery, barking up a storm. People were shrieking and jumping out of the way as Royal raced through the crowd. I ran as fast as I could, but the dog was on a mission, and once he made it to the graveside, he went straight after Franklin Fogg.

I didn't waste time calling out for the dog again, instead I shouldered my way past the people who had stopped to gawk at the spectacle. Christy was right beside me when I finally managed to grab ahold of the trailing end of Royal's bedazzled leash.

"Royal, heel!" I said, trying to pull him off Franklin and the people who were gathered around him.

But the dog was having none of it. His growls were low and mean and he seemed to be herding Franklin and Alicia's brother back.

"Royal stop!" I gave his leash a sharp pull and it seemed to snap the dog out of his attack mode.

The pug glanced back at me, and I knelt down. "Come here, boy." I tried to sound soothing. "It's okay."

Royal shook himself and trotted over. I shortened the leash and cautiously patted the dog. He leaned against my legs and made a whining sound.

I steeled myself and met Franklin Fogg's red, angry face. "I'm sorry Franklin. He got loose and—"

"You, again!" he snapped, and proceeded to launch into a tirade at top volume.

I felt Christy's hand drop on my shoulder. "Stay cool, Nilah." She gave my shoulder a bolstering squeeze. "Back-up has arrived."

Detective Dennis Tucker walked onto the scene. "Everyone just settle down," he said.

Royal decided to act adorable for the moment and sat in the wet grass with his tongue hanging out. If I wouldn't have known better, I'd have sworn the dog winked at me.

"I told you to stay away from the funeral!" Franklin shouted.

"Calm down, Franklin," Devin James said. "Clearly the woman wants the publicity and the attention from disrupting a private family funeral. Don't let her win."

Alicia's brother was impeccably dressed. He hovered at Franklin's side, and I was surprised when he ran his gloved hand possessively down Franklin's arm. *Not unlike a lover would,* I realized.

I shook the thoughts off. "I'm not trying to get any publicity," I argued. "Franklin, I apologize for the disruption. The dog jumped out of the car and I tried to catch him—"

"Officer!" Franklin pointed at me. "I want

this woman arrested!"

"On what charge?" Christy laughed in his face. "For having a dog in a public place?"

"How dare you!" Franklin's face turned an alarming shade of purple and he stepped forward.

Royal began to growl at the sudden movement, and Franklin jumped back.

I saw a foot shoot out and I recoiled from what would have surely been a kick in the face, but Royal jumped into action. He snapped at the incoming shoe, and somehow blocked the blow. I ended up landing on my butt in the wet grass.

"Hey!" Christy yelled at Devin James who'd unsuccessfully tried to kick either me, or the dog. She put her whole body between us and the men, and gave the blonde man a hard shove. "What the hell is wrong with you?" she demanded.

"Assault!" Devin James screamed. "She put her hands on me. You all saw it!"

"That's it." Detective Tucker broke Christy and the man apart. "Ms. Stefanik, you and your friend should take the dog back to the car. Mr.

Fogg, you and your companion both need to calm down and cool off."

"But she—"

"Enough!" the detective's voice was tough as nails. "I witnessed you attempting to kick Ms. Stefanik in the face. If anyone will have charges for assault pressed against them today, it might be *you*, Mr. James."

Christy gave my arm a tug and helped me climb to my feet. Royal made one more lunge at Mr. Pretentious, who practically jumped into Franklin's arms, and I half-heartedly pulled the dog back. "Let's go, Royal," I said, but ended up having to drag the growling pug away from the men. It wasn't easy.

I'd managed to put a little distance between us and them, and Christy reached over for Royal's leash. "Here," she said. "Let me." With one low command and a strong tug, my friend had the dog heeling at her side again.

"Whoa, it's the dog whisperer," I said, impressed with her neat handling of the unruly dog.

"You feel sorry for him too much," Christy said briskly. "He needs—"

"Please don't say: rules, boundaries and limitations."

Christy rolled her eyes. "I was going to say a firm hand." She waited a beat. "Speaking of which...who was the posh, metrosexual dude hanging all over Franklin?"

"That's Alicia's brother. Devin James. He's been in the papers."

"Oh, that's why he was familiar. I think I've seen him on the news too." Christy leaned in closer. "So, is Franklin gay?"

I sent her a withering look. "He was married. To Alicia. Remember?"

"He was married to the biggest bitch on the east coast, and I truly can't imagine those two ever knocking boots." She wiggled her eyebrows. "Besides, they never had any kids. Maybe Alicia was his beard."

I kept my voice low. "Franklin's a pretentious jerk, no doubt about it. But behave yourself." I did my best not to smile. "We're in a cemetery, this is no time to be cracking jokes."

"Hey, I'm not judging him. I'm more like, 'Go get some of that, Franklin!'" Christy nudged me. "You *did* catch the body language between those two, right?"

"I did." I blew out a breath and reminded myself that giggling was not appropriate while they were literally burying someone a few feet away.

"That whole scene was *very* interesting, I'm telling you." Christy pitched her voice even lower. "And Alicia's brother? He puts me in mind of a man searching for a sugar daddy."

A laugh escaped despite my best efforts, and I tried to change it into a cough. "Thanks for that mental image, Christy."

"You're welcome." Christy grinned. "Made you laugh, though."

I was still smiling when Christy put Royal in my car with a minimum of fuss. I didn't mind when she ordered me to drive straight to DPI. I eased my car on to the gravel road, saw that Christy was right behind me in her black Nissan, and drove sedately out of the cemetery.

I'd pulled to a stop at an intersection when Royal started whining. I patted his homely head. "What's wrong, buddy?" I checked rearview, intending to wave to Christy, and jolted.

The spirit of Alicia Fogg was sitting in my backseat.

"God damn it, Alicia!" I swore. "You scared me! Why are you still here?"

"Because we're not finished yet."

"What the hell is that supposed to mean?" I asked as Royal gave a joyful bark and leapt into the back seat.

Alicia did a face-palm. "I *told* you to hit the books."

"So that whole book display *was* from you. How'd you manage to get past my wards to do that anyway?"

"Perhaps I should have left you a note written in crayons." Alicia mimed writing. "You know, in big block letters. Something simple and to the point."

"I read the dream dictionary. I get it. I'm in danger."

"Well, sweet hallelujah! After two attempts on your life, you've finally figured it out!" Alicia tossed up her hands. "I've often thought you weren't very bright, Nilah."

The light was still red, so I twisted and

looked over my shoulder. "Listen, I've had enough of your condescending bullshit, lady."

Royal sat beside the image of his mistress. He lifted a paw towards the spirit, and when he couldn't touch her he began to whine louder than before.

"I'm sorry," Alicia said. "I didn't mean to upset you. You're the closest thing to a friend I've ever had."

Caught off guard by the sincerity of her tone, I tried to be civil. "Well, thank you for apologizing."

Alicia sneered. "I was speaking to the dog. Not to you."

"Of course you were." I shook my head.

Alicia tried unsuccessfully to fix her hair. "Well, come to think of it, you and I do have a sort of *working relationship*, I suppose. I'd hesitate to call you a friend, however."

"Priceless." I muttered, wondering why I'd ever thought the woman capable of any sort of empathy for another human being.

"Have I offended you?" Alicia asked.

I banged my fists on the steering wheel out of sheer frustration. "Why can't you cross over and leave me alone?"

"I have no idea." She folded her arms over her chest. "All I do know is that you still have more to do."

"That's fucking fantastic." The light changed to green and I switched my attention to the road.

"This dog leash is new," Alicia said, changing topics. "It's bedazzled, and completely ridiculous."

"My sister bought it for him," I said. "She's crazy for Royal. Her little girl, Vanda, likes him too."

Suddenly, Alicia appeared beside me in the front passenger seat. "How was Royal around the little one?"

"He was awesome, actually."

"I knew he would be," Alicia sighed. "I always wanted children."

"No way." I glanced over at her. "You? Seriously?"

"Yes, I did. But Franklin didn't."

A thought bounced into my head. "Can I ask you something? Seeing as we're *friends* and all."

"God help me," Alicia groaned. "I've become friends with a Gypsy."

"How the mighty have fallen."

"I probably deserve that." Alicia actually smiled at me. "So what's your question, friend?"

I smiled in return. "It's probably rude."

Alicia smirked even as her image began to fade. "A lack of manners has never stopped you before."

"Is Franklin gay?" I blurted it out quickly, before she disappeared.

Alicia burst out laughing, and was gone.

CHAPTER TEN

By the time we arrived at Beth's house, I was freezing. My car smelled like wet dog, and I was a bit flustered from my visit with Alicia. The rain had picked back up as soon as I parked, so Royal and I made a run for the back door with Christy right on our heels.

Since my jeans were soaked, Beth let me borrow a pair of her baggy sweat pants, which fit my curves more like skin tight leggings. They weren't comfortable, but they'd do in a pinch.

I walked out into the office and stopped in my tracks. "I was supposed to bring lunch."

Beth took my damp clothes to toss them in her dryer. "Christy called me after you both left the funeral," she said. "I ordered delivery. It'll be here in a half hour."

"I'm sorry, Beth," I said. "At least let me pay for it."

"I've got it. No worries." Beth patted my arm. "Go have a seat. I want to hear all about everything that's been happening."

I settled in my office chair, and when Beth came back I filled my friends in while Christy dried off Royal with an old towel. First, I told Beth about Royal disrupting the graveside service.

"Why was Franklin so angry that *you* were there?" Beth asked.

"I should probably tell you what happened a week ago..." I said, and gave them both the rundown on my close encounter with Franklin the day that Vanessa had gone to the ER.

Beth wasn't pleased. "You should have let detective Tucker know that Franklin had confronted you."

"He didn't *confront* me—"

"It's too coincidental!" Beth cut me off. "He conveniently happens to be jogging in Joseph's neighborhood and a short time later that car jumped the curb and almost hit you."

I thought back to how I'd lost track of Franklin right before Vanessa had called me. I gulped. "There's more."

"More?" Christy's eyes narrowed.

"Yeah," I admitted. "Alicia graced me with another visitation. It happened on the drive over."

Christy shuddered. "I saw you look over your shoulder, on the drive here...but I figured you were talking to the dog in the backseat."

"Nope, it was Alicia. Again." I pushed up from my chair and began to pace. "I'm tired of all of this! I want my life back!" I realized I was shouting and didn't really care. "Everything has been insane since I followed Alicia's ghost and found her body."

Beth reached out and stopped my pacing with a hand on my arm. "In retrospect, traipsing off in the woods alone wasn't your brightest move."

Her words, so like Alicia's, annoyed the hell out of me. "Yeah, no kidding!" I snarked. "I never thought about what would happen afterwards. All I wanted was some peace—"

"I'd say that backfired on you," Beth said,

interrupting my rant. "Instead you became a person of interest to the police and the media."

"Getting interrogated at the police station and chased by reporters hasn't exactly been the high points of my life." I dropped back in my chair.

"Have you considered that *you* may be the one keeping Alicia tethered to this plane?" Christy asked quietly.

"What do you mean by that exactly?" I said, surprised by her switch in topics.

"I'm wondering if your frustration at the situation is feeding the spirit. Making for a tighter bond." Christy's eyes were intense as she studied me. "She's so desperate to make contact with anyone who cares, that she managed to get past the wards at your place."

I flinched. "Alicia practically admitted that I was the only friend she'd ever had..."

"To be fair, you have tried to help her, and she *has* made attempts to warn you," Christy said. "Now, while I applaud the effort, you need to let her go, Nilah. Cut the psychic ties. Then you both can be at peace."

"Are you saying that *I'm* the only one who

can get her to move on—cross over?"

Christy nodded. "I believe so. You need to make a symbolic gesture, an act of release and closing. That should do the trick."

"Okay," I said, thinking it over. "Maybe I could leave some flowers at her grave and wish her safe passage on her way to the other side."

"That would be very a thoughtful gesture." Beth smiled.

"Something simple," Christy suggested. "I'd go for doing it at sunset. Close of the day and all."

"Yeah, I get that," I said. "I could take a little bouquet of fall flowers to the cemetery, and leave it for her."

"Chrysanthemums would be an excellent choice," Christy said. "According to flower folklore they help keep wandering spirits away."

"Really?" I perked up. "I think I have a new favorite flower."

"Girlfriend," Christy chuckled. "I am never bored with you in my life."

"I do feel a little more empowered, sort of, with a plan in place," I admitted. "But the whole situation is crazy, and this past week has been insane. I made some poor choices, and I'm still not sure why I didn't end up sitting in a jail cell."

"You had both me and Rick to corroborate your alibi." Beth ticked off the reasons on her fingers. "There was no physical evidence. You really didn't fit the profile, or even have a good motive."

I rolled my eyes. "Except that she'd fired me last year."

"Not liking someone isn't a motive, and if it was the police have an entire town to question." Christy pointed out. "Because I don't think *anyone* else in town truly cared for her either. Beth, you should have seen the 'expressions' on the mourners' faces today."

"How do you mean?" Beth wanted to know.

"They looked irritated, not grief stricken," I explained.

"That's awful," Beth said, and picked up the local paper from her desk. "Especially when you consider that someone leaked to the press that the cause of Alicia's death was strangulation."

A few seconds of silence hung over our office. Finally I spoke up. "So it was murder."

"Strangulation?" Christy asked, taking the paper from Beth. "That's a pretty *personal* way to take someone out. Considering you'd be up in their face while you killed them."

Her words had me flashing back to the day I found Alicia's body. It was almost as if a series of still photos shuffled through my mind. And as they did, I remembered something. "She fought back." I heard myself say. "Her nails were chipped and torn up. I saw that when I found her body."

Christy continued to scan the newspaper article. "Do they say in the article whether or not they have any physical evidence?"

Beth shook her head. "I'd say it's a safe bet they did collect some, and I'm sure that the police know much more than they are letting on."

I studied Beth. "So you're saying they *are* gathering evidence, maybe even have a real suspect in mind?"

"According to the paper and the interview with his attorney, Franklin has only been questioned." Christy peered over the top of the pages. "It seems to me that the writer of the article is *alluding* that Franklin is a suspect. He hasn't been formally charged with anything."

Beth leaned back in her chair. "Yeah, but let's be honest. There's been a few other circumstances and events for the police to consider with this case, as well."

"Such as?" I asked.

At Beth's nod it was Christy who spoke. "The gas leak at your building."

I frowned. "But we were told it was old, faulty equipment..."

Christy snorted. "I call bullshit. My gut says it was tampered with."

"Tampered with?" The enormity of that statement hit me hard.

"Nilah." Christy took my hand. "Don't you get it? Someone came after you, twice."

"Twice?"

"By the Goddess, Nilah." Christy squeezed my hand. "How could you *not* put the clues together? You are supposed to be a psychic."

"Well I'm not a psychic, *or* a detective for that matter," I argued. "I'm a medium who's still learning. I've been dealing with an annoying ghost who tends to follow me around bitching non-stop every time I step out of my house!" I heard the petulance in my own voice and stopped. "God." I drug a hand through my hair. "Now I'm even starting to sound like her."

"That's a side effect from the energetic ties," Christy said. "I forget sometimes that you didn't come into your gifts until last year. But Nilah, I'm worried that the killer is trying to tie up loose ends. Your name and picture has been all over the paper. The story last year about recovering the jewelry has been making the rounds again, and now with you finding Alicia..." Christy held up the front page.

I took the paper from her. The headline read, 'Local Psychic Finds Body Of Missing Woman'. Much farther down the front page was a photo of Alicia, clipped from some society column, no doubt. In noticeably smaller print the header read: 'Funeral For Alicia James-Fogg Held Today'.

I'd been avoiding the papers for the past week. However, seeing the current headlines gave me a hell of a jolt. *They'd called me a psychic not a medium,* I realized, staring at the page in horror. "Most people figure that if an individual has one psychic talent..." I gulped and made myself finish the sentence. "That they should have them all. Which means there's a good chance that the killer assumes if I was able to find the body then I would know who he —or she was."

"Nilah, you've put yourself in a very precarious position." Beth sighed.

"Christy, would it be presumptuous of me to ask you for a protection spell?"

"I worked one for you this morning." Christy reached into her purse and handed me a small purple fabric bag. "Here, take this. The sachet bag is filled with protective herbs, and crystals. Keep it on your person at all times."

A knock on the back door had all three of us flinching. "It's the lunch delivery," Beth said. "I've got it."

Mentally prying my fingernails from the ceiling, I flashed a smile to my friends and tried to act like I *wasn't* terrified. Beth passed out the little containers of soup and the sandwiches. Royal sat and shamelessly begged at Beth's side. I went for the soup, thinking it might sit better on my nervous stomach.

We finished our lunch and Christy went back to her shop. Beth had an interview for a prospective haunt investigation, and I promised to stay put at the office. I locked the door behind her and set the alarms. A short time afterwards I was able to put my dry jeans back on, and out of desperation, I dove into answering the DPI email to keep myself busy.

After a few hours of work, I gave up and pulled out a legal pad. While Royal gnawed on his tennis ball, I tried to write up a little something, as Christy had suggested. A statement of intent, essentially. After working with both Beth and Christy for the past year, I'd picked up some basic information about the paranormal and magick. I knew that magick was all about the *intent* of the practitioner. And I had a pretty good idea of what to do.

I drafted out a few things, keeping it short and simple. I deliberately let the events of the past week play back through my mind. All of it. From first discovering Alicia in my apartment, Royal showing up, and finding the body. I winced over the police interrogations, the intrusion of the press, the gas leak, my confrontation with Franklin, the close call with the car, and then today's fiasco at the cemetery.

I'd been damn lucky, I thought, watching the pug who was now chasing his ball around the office. *Or maybe, I'd been protected from the onset.*

As if he knew where my thoughts were, Royal trotted over. He rose up, resting his paws on my thigh, and dropped the slobbery ball in my lap. "Hey Royal," I said, and the bug-eyed dog nudged my side with his nose. "Your Mistress seems to have been working overtime since her death, trying to help me."

Royal cocked his head to one side, and his whole butt began to wiggle.

"Yeah, you certainly have too. You're like a super dog." I assured him. "Now it's my turn to help her. So she can be at peace." I ruffled the dog's ears and reached for my cell phone.

However, I was certainly not going to go do this alone. I tapped on the screen for the number of my sexy man-beast.

He didn't even say hello. "Nilah, are you

okay?" was his opening line.

I smiled. "I am," I promised him. "I'm here at the office, but I was wondering if you would help me out with a little something."

"What are you up to now?" Joseph asked, sounding suspicious.

"It's only an errand. I need to say goodbye to a friend."

***

Dusk was falling and the rain had finally stopped when Joseph pulled his truck over to the side of the gravel road in the cemetery. He switched the engine off and we sat in the cab silently for a few moments.

"You sure that you're up for this?" he asked.

"I am." I said, picking up the little bouquet of fall flowers from my lap. "This feels right to me."

"I'm glad that you called, you shouldn't be out here alone, considering everything."

I reached over and gave his arm a squeeze through his work jacket. "I'm just relieved that you aren't weirded out by this."

"It takes more than you talking to ghosts to freak me out, babe." Joseph covered my hand with his. "It's you messing around with crime scenes that makes me nervous."

"I'm sorry about that." I kissed his cheek. "Trust me when I say I've learned my lesson. No more following ghosts into the woods, or searching for bodies."

"Are you ready?" he asked.

I buttoned up my green coat. "Let's do this." I let myself out the passenger door and waited for Joseph to walk around to my side of the vehicle. We were alone in the cemetery, and after looping my arm through his, together we started off towards Alicia's burial site.

There was a mountain of flowers arranged over the fresh mound of dirt. I studied the little grocery store chrysanthemums wrapped in their crinkly cellophane and took a deep breath to psych myself up. Joseph gave my arm a bolstering squeeze and let me go.

I stepped forward alone. "Alicia James-Fogg, I hope you will be at rest now," I said. "If I truly was the closest thing you ever had to a friend, then be at peace knowing that a friend found you, and made sure you were taken home." I crouched down and set the flowers at the base of the other arrangements. "With these words, I now sever any and all energetic links or psychic ties we may have had. I wish you well on your journey to the other side."

I felt a funny little ping in the center of my solar plexus and I sucked my breath in hard. I had to drop a knee to the damp grass to keep my balance, and as I knelt there I experienced the oddest sensation. I could *feel* the energetic links breaking, and my heart grew lighter.

It was over almost as soon as it began, and I rose to my feet. I waited, but when nothing else happened, I stepped back with Joseph and took his arm again. "I think that did it," I blew out a long breath.

I tipped my face up to his, relieved and happy, but Joseph wasn't looking at me. Instead he was staring intently to his right. I swung my gaze over and saw a man easing around the nearby trunk of a large tree.

Joseph shifted, putting himself between me and the man.

My heart dropped. "You *can* see him, right?"

I asked softly.

"There's a man wearing a brown jacket." Joseph said out of the side of his mouth. "He showed up when you were placing the flowers."

"That's Devin James, Alicia's brother." I said, torn between relief that it was a living person, and alarm at the man skulking around. "Devin, are you alright?" I called over.

"No, I'm not." Devin was staggering like a drunk. "Because you've ruined everything."

"Stay back," Joseph growled at the man. "I won't tell you twice."

"You don't tell me what to do!" Devin said, even as he stumbled to a halt. He swayed on his feet, looking way up to meet Joseph's eyes. "My sister couldn't simply die and leave me in peace, could she?"

"Is he drunk?" I asked Joseph. "What's wrong with him?"

"Nilah." Joseph shifted positions, and his voice was low and urgent. "Get behind me."

Recognizing the fighter's stance, I immediately backed up, giving my man plenty of room. "Be careful Joseph," I said. "That guy is seriously screwed up."

Devin heard me and snapped his shoulders back, clearly offended. "Freaking Gypsy trash —you can't talk to me that way!"

"Well, we just did." Joseph smiled even as he taunted the man. "What are you going to do about it, *suka*?"

Devin snarled and rushed forward.

Joseph snapped out a fist, connecting with Devin James' chin. The smaller man's head rocked back and he landed on his ass next to the fresh grave.

"Stay down," Joseph ordered him.

"Well, damn, honey." I whistled. "That short punch was impressive."

"Thanks, babe." Joseph nodded. "Who should we call for him? He seems drunk, or high."

Reaching in my coat pocket for my cell, I cautiously kept my eyes on Devin. He remained on the grass, but he lifted his hands, grabbed his own hair, and began to pull on it.

Alicia's spirit unexpectedly appeared beside her brother. "Alicia's here,' I told Joseph, and was shocked when I could see my own breath puff out on the air.

Joseph shivered. "Whoa, the temperature really dropped."

"I think she's causing that."

Joseph took my arm. "Where is she?"

"She's standing right beside him," was all I could manage. Alicia appeared different from any other time I'd seen her. Her hair was down, flowing, and she seemed for lack of a better word—determined.

Alicia reached down to touch her brother. "Devin," she said.

Devin swung his head around, focused on her and screamed in terror. Causing both Joseph and I to jump.

"He can see her," I managed.

"So can I, now." Joseph's voice was strained.

"I'll bet that's because she wants you to." I whispered, shivering in the cold caused by the spirit.

Devin scrambled back away from the apparition. "You can't be here! You're dead. I killed you!"

"Shit, call the police," Joseph whispered to me.

"I'm dialing now." I eased back, making the

call as quietly as possible.

"Why, Devin?" Alicia said. "Why did you do this?"

"You deserved it! You always had everything, and you never cared about anyone else! Only yourself!"

"That's not true." Alicia shook her head. "I paid for you to go to school, but I cut you off when you got involved with drugs. You need help, Devin."

"This isn't happening. You can't be here." Devon yanked brutally on his own hair again. "It's the damn Gypsy. The psychic that found your body!" Devin screamed. "*She's* making me see all this."

While I was on the phone, speaking softly to the 911 operator, Devin began rocking himself back and forth. "I tried scaring the psychic off," he announced.

"How'd you try and scare her off?" Joseph asked, cautiously.

"The gas line at the apartments...didn't mean for that to get so bad." Devin's voice was apologetic, almost reasonable sounding, and that made it far more terrifying.

"Please tell me you can hear this," I said to the operator, and switched my phone over to 'speaker'. I held it out, hoping they would be able to hear Devin clearly.

"And the car," Devin suddenly added. "I didn't really want to hurt her, only scare the stupid Gypsy into shutting up. You know?"

"Did you catch that?" I asked the 911 operator.

"Yes ma'am we did,' she said. "Stay on the line. Help will be there any moment, now."

"They're on the way," I repeated to Joseph, staying beside him.

"Good." Joseph slanted his eyes over to mine.

Devin folded his arms across his middle, and seemed to completely break down. He continued to rock back and forth, crying and babbling to himself. From the distance I began to hear police sirens.

Alicia lifted her head and smiled at Joseph and me. "Thank you, Nilah." Her apparition seemed to glow with a brighter light.

I nodded. "You're welcome."

"Take good care of Royal," she said.

"I will," I promised, and in the blink of an eye she was gone.

"Amazing," Joseph murmured.

I let my breath out slowly. "What do we do now?" I asked Joseph.

"We wait for the police." Joseph continued to keep an eye on Devin, even as the sound of the police cars drew closer. "Please, stand behind me. I want you far away from this guy."

For once I didn't argue. Wrapping my fingers around the hem of my lover's coat, I held on and kept an eye on the entrance to the cemetery. It wasn't long before several squad cars came tearing into the graveyard parking lot.

I gave Joseph's jacket a tug. "The cavalry has arrived."

"Finally." Joseph's shoulders dropped slightly.

The police rushed in and secured Devin James quickly. While Joseph and I moved back I suddenly remembered the phone. "Ma'am?" I disengaged the speaker and tucked the phone under my ear. "The police are here and they have him."

I disconnected, and heard mine and Joseph's

names being called. I recognized the officer immediately, and gave Rick Casper a wave even as he ran to us.

"Are you both alright?" he demanded.

"We're fine, Rick,' I assured him.

Joseph clapped Rick on the shoulder. "Good to see you, man."

"What the hell happened?" Rick asked.

"Oh you know, it's a regular night. Hanging out at the cemetery with my girl." Joseph's eyes crinkled at the corners.

Rick barked out a laugh, told us to stay put, and went off to speak to another officer.

I tucked my arm under Joseph's coat and gave him a one-armed hug. "You saw your first ghost," I said. "Are you doing okay?"

"I actually saw *and* heard her." Joseph shuddered. "That was intense!"

"Welcome to my world." I added a little squeeze. "Can I show a guy a good time, or what?"

Joseph tilted his head back and studied the sky. "I swear to god woman, you need a keeper."

"Oh yeah?" I raised my eyebrows at him,

"Do you have someone specific in mind?"

"Yeah, as a matter of fact, I do." Joseph looked down in to my eyes. "Marry me, Nilah."

"*What*?" I almost fell over.

"Marry me," he repeated as the police bustled around us.

I couldn't help it, I started to laugh. "Joseph Serafin, you picked a hell of a time to propose."

Joseph shrugged. "Seems like the perfect time to me."

"Well, I—"

"I love you," he said, cutting me off.

My lips twitched, but I planted my hands on my hips. "You'd better have a ring."

"As a matter of fact, I have it at the house."

I smiled. "Good answer."

He stood, grinning at me. My sexy man-beast with his long hair resting on those broad shoulders, and a devilish twinkle in his brown eyes. "So, what do you have to say?" he asked.

"Yes," I said, and launched myself at him. "I'll marry you!"

EPILOGUE

It took a while to straighten everything out. We ended up in the police department for a few hours giving our statements. Officer Rick Casper had called Beth—who called Christy. She in turn contacted my family, and they all descended on us like the wrath of god.

When we announced that we were engaged, the place went a little crazy.

I don't think I've ever been sworn at, cried over, or hugged so much in such a short period of time.

The local newspapers had a field day over the circumstances surrounding Devin James' confession. Eventually the furor died down and Franklin made a statement to the press. He even thanked me for helping to bring his wife's killer to justice. Best of all, the little ritual I had done to sever any psychic ties the night Devin was arrested seemed to have worked. Alicia's spirit had truly crossed over.

Royal is retired from the dog show circuit. He now has a forever home with Vanessa, Tony, and little Vanda. I imagine that he's going to be spoiled rotten and have bedazzled leashes for the rest of his life. The last time I visited my sister's house, the pug was snuggled up next to my niece while she napped on a quilt on the floor. Alicia, I knew, would have been very pleased with the arrangement for her beloved dog.

Squash and I moved with Joseph into the little house he inherited from his grandfather. Christy helped me to ward the hell out of it, so no paranormal visitors will come a-calling. Yes, I still work full-time at the offices of DPI, and if I do consult as a medium for the paranormal team, it's done privately. I've learned my lesson about stumbling onto crime scenes, and my Nancy Drew days are over.

Besides, we have a wedding to plan.

My sister, both of our mothers, and my grandmother were all happy and excited about the wedding preparations. While Joseph and I considered venues, and settled on a color scheme, Vanessa, Beth, and Christy all debated the pros and cons of fabric swatches for their bridesmaid dresses.

My mother had some great ideas for table decorations. However, I insisted that chrysanthemums be a part of the centerpieces, and all the bridal party flowers—especially my bouquet. I want to make damn sure that any roaming ghosts stay far away from me on our big day.

The biggest surprise of all our planning was when my grandmother informed me that she needed a plus one for the wedding. She and Detective Dennis Tucker are dating. I told her that makes her a cougar—as she's several years older than the man.

Her response was that she didn't mind having a younger lover because, "the sex" was absolutely spectacular.

That'll teach me to mouth off to my *babcia.*

The End

ABOUT THE AUTHOR

Ellen Dugan is the award winning author of over twenty five books. Ellen's popular non-fiction titles have been translated into over twelve foreign languages. She branched out successfully into paranormal fiction in 2015 with her popular "Legacy Of Magick" series, and has been featured in USA TODAY'S HEA column. Ellen lives an enchanted life in Missouri. Please visit her website and blog:

www.ellendugan.com
www.ellendugan.blogspot.com

Polish words and pronunciation

Babcia (Bahp-chya) — Grandmother

Ddzień dobry (Jean Dough-bree) — Good Morning

Duch- (doohk) — ghost or spirit

Dobra czarownica (dobrah tarov-nee-saa) — good witch

Dziadzio (Jah-joh) — Grandpa

Dupek (doo-peck) — asshole

Dziękuję (Jin-gwe chi) — thank you

Kocham cię (ko-hahm tchiem) — I love you

Kochanie (Ko-han-yeh) — Darling

Kretyn (kreh-tin) — jerk

Magia (mahg-ya) — magick

Miłego dnia (Mee-uego dne-ea) — Have a nice day

Polska Roma (Polska Romah) — Romany Gypsy from Poland

Psychiczna średniej (Psa-he-chna shred-nyee) — Psychic medium

Śmieć (Schmechee) — trash

Suka (soo-kah) — bitch

Upiór (Oo-pee-orra) — phantom, spook, ghoul

Wnucka (vnoochka) — Granddaughter

Made in the USA
Monee, IL
20 June 2022

98322438R00105